THE SPIDER:
THE DEVIL'S DEATH DWARFS

THE
MASTER OF MEN!

SPIDER®

THE DEVIL'S
DEATH DWARFS

By Grant Stockbridge

STEEGER BOOKS • 2020

CHAPTER 1
THE SECOND TERROR

T HE SECOND descent of the Terror upon the Western World caught even Richard Wentworth unprepared. Recovering from wounds suffered in his last battle against the Man from the East, still hiding out from the police, Wentworth had felt reasonably secure. He had been sure that Tang-akhmut would never again lead his power-drunk cohorts against mankind. For Tang-akhmut was in the death house at Sing Sing, to which Wentworth had sent him. Within twenty-four hours, Tang-akhmut would pay for the massacres that had almost made him master of the great city of New York. That was on the fifth of September. On the night of the sixth....

The horror of the Terror's second coming, its descent upon the Middle West, crowded even the news of Tang-akhmut's escape from Sing Sing off the front pages of newspapers. In a single night, death in horrid form had been visited upon a dozen widely scattered homes in Cincinnati, Ohio. What made the crimes more awful—aside from the maniacal cruelty with which men and women had been tortured to death—was the utter lack of any intelligible reason for the attacks.—And the hysterical refusal of the surviving victims—the loved ones who had been forced to witness the tortures—to tell the police what had happened or who was responsible!

To be sure, there was no evidence that Tang-akhmut was

instituting the Terror. It was even doubtful if the sinister Egyptian, fleeing Sing Sing, could have reached Ohio in time to have participated in the crimes. But Wentworth, hearing the almost

These were the men of Tang-akhmut,

kidnaping the chosen victims.

panicky voices of radio announcers, reading the hysterical outcry of the newspapers, had no doubt at all. In some way, working from his death cell, Tang-akhmut had planned these atrocities.

He had timed them so that a city prostrate in terror awaited his terrible second coming— And there was no hesitancy in Richard Wentworth's response. Within the hour, he was speeding westward by plane.

Even that first step of his second battle with Tang-akhmut was hampered. Not only was he a fugitive from charges of murder framed very perfectly by Tang-akhmut, but he had been stripped of all his wealth by the man's machinations. He had been forced to eke out a meager living by preying upon crooks and had operated with the greatest difficulty under the increased vigilance of the danger-stimulated police. Now, speeding to match strength with the man who possessed what undoubtedly was the greatest criminal brain it had been the misfortune of the world to spawn, Wentworth traveled alone, with scarcely a hundred dollars in his pockets, and totally without reserves....

Wentworth found terror a tangible thing in the streets of Cincinnati. Even in the thick heat of noon, it was obvious. Men moved furtively or with a jerky bravado about their work, and women showed themselves only in huddled, hurrying groups. The police patrolled their beats in pairs, guns in hand. Already the city had learned that no man could say when the next blow would fall, nor where it would strike. The very hours of Wentworth's westward race had brought forth a fresh tale of frightfulness. The daughter of an apparently insignificant physician had been horribly tortured before his eyes and afterwards the mangled parts of a girl's body had been strewn through the city. Reasonless, maniacal and frightful—Yet Wentworth knew that Tang-akhmut never struck without reason!

He threw himself into the battle. And within an hour after glimpsing the Terror that stalked the streets of the city, Wentworth himself felt the power of the Egyptian's sinister hand!

Wentworth saw his course clearly before him. Regardless of how closely it might associate him with the police, or the perpetual risk of discovery and arrest, he must go directly to the home of the bereaved physician. The newspapers gave Dr. Zachary Abel a glowing write-up, told of his thousand benevolences among the poor to whom he devoted himself. The daughter who had been tortured, Willa Abel, had been a minor clerk in a city department. A niece, Clare Hubbell, assisted Abel in his medical work. The papers and the police pored over these meager facts, seeking a reason, a motive for the attack. To some crimes, police found answers. A banker had been forced by the torture of his wife to manipulate the time-lock on his vault; a jeweler had been similarly constrained with his son as a victim. A wealthy stockholder had been compelled to ransom his daughter from the torturers by a payment that pauperized him—and afterward his daughter had been wantonly killed. But, for the tormenting of Willa Abel and her father, there seemed no explanation at all....

There were two courses open to Wentworth. He had prepared forged credentials which would identify him as Oscar Franzen, a police detective from New York City. He had disguised himself to fill that role so that he could go to the Cincinnati police and learn what had been accomplished. But that would involve him in constant danger of discovery. It seemed better to hold that in reserve and go, alone, to the assistance of Dr. Abel. If he could catch a hint of Tang-akhmut's hidden motive....

THE DOOR of the apartment house offered no obstacle to Wentworth's skilled fingers and the lock of the silent suite which the Abels occupied yielded with equal ease. Better to come upon the doctor secretly. Surprise had its value, even when the invasion was kindly meant.

Standing poised in the dim foyer on the apartment, Wentworth sent his swift glance over the interior. The living room had the shabby homeliness of the man who owned it. A roll-top desk in a corner was flanked by a battered leather chair. There were stacks of books… Wentworth whirled to the door behind him. A hand had tried the knob and now, in distant reaches of the apartment, the door bell was buzzing! The devil! Had he been spotted entering the building? No—his entrance had been nothing to excite attention and no one had seen his swift climb up the steps to this floor. Then… had he been followed here by Tang-akhmut? It was not beyond the genius of the man that he had spotted Wentworth, even in disguise! He would be sure Wentworth would hasten to the battle call, and he could watch arrivals. It would be like his subtlety thus to ring the doorbell and effect a quiet entrance….

A girl's slow footsteps moving toward him through the apartment sent Wentworth leaping toward the only unobvious cover that the room afforded. Within seconds, he was crouched in the tunneled opening under the roll-top desk. He found that his hand was on the butt of one of the twin automatics that nestled in holsters beneath his arms and it brought his lips grimly together. If these were the agents of Tang-akhmut….

No hope of personal vengeance had driven Wentworth into

this mad dash westward. There was no place in this man for the pettiness of such rancor. But his life was pledged to a great cause, the defense of the people. Always the men of his family had served the country they loved in some capacity, but none had  chosen a greater field than the last of the Wentworth line. Richard Wentworth had chosen to battle the most bitterly menacing of modern threats to civilization, the mounting power of organized crime. And to do that, he had found it necessary to work outside the law, to become at times a criminal, to be his own court and executioner of men too great, too clever, for legal forces to entrap. In the end, he had created secretly an identity from whose very name criminals shrank in fear. He had become a knight errant of justice, striking always in the cause of humanity against crime. He had named himself the Spider.

And because he had occasionally stepped outside the law to effect the ends of justice, because his swift guns had sometimes served the purpose of a hangman's rope, the Spider was a hunted man with a huge price on his head.

The girl who came to answer that summons at the door entered the room where Wentworth crouched, moved heavily across his line of vision. There was a droop in her young body, an intolerable weight upon her shoulders, but her head was still bravely erect. She stood with her hand on the door, called a clear question, then manipulated the lock. A man bounded through….

"Clare! Clare!" he cried. "Oh, thank God, dear… You are still safe!"

Slowly, Wentworth lowered his automatic to his side, a smile tugging at his mouth corners, a smile that held only gentleness and sympathy for the girl and boy locked in each other's arms there by the door.

"Oh, Adam!" The girl called Clare was sobbing now, her brave golden head bowed at last.

Wentworth waited a while before he stepped clear of the hiding place and, gun hanging at his side, confronted the two.

"I am here to help you," he said quietly.

With a thrust, the man hurled Clare from him. His hand darted across his body in a gesture Wentworth knew, reaching for a hidden gun.

"Hold it!" Wentworth snapped, leveling his own weapon. "Perhaps you didn't understand. I said that I was here to help you!"

His gun hand tensely ready, the man froze in a rigid posture of defense. There was strain in his drawn cheeks.

"Put that gun down," the man ordered. "I am Detective Peck, city police! And you can tell your two pals to come out of hiding. This building is surrounded!"

The man's order stopped words on Wentworth's lips. He had been on the point of revealing himself. Men might fear the Spider, but at least they knew that he fought criminals. They might be glad to enlist his powerful aid. And, his real identity secure in disguise, Wentworth had thought it best to announce himself as the Spider and proffer help. But with the building surrounded by police… It was not that thought at which his mind leaped. Detective Adam Peck had said *you can tell your two pals…* Only one interpretation of that. Three men had been seen to enter the building together. Peck thought Wentworth one of them, but the truth was a more sinister thing. Three men had entered the building on Wentworth's heels, three men who perhaps were *agents of Tang-akhmut!*

CHAPTER 2
THE GLITTERING DEATH

WENTWORTH'S CERTAINTY of the identity of the three who had entered the apartment building was quicker than any analysis, faster than reasoned deduction. The constant pressure of peril had given him this swift faculty, but the basis of his guess that the three men were agents of Tang-akhmut was plain. The police were on guard over the building and were suspicious of the trio, therefore they must be alien to the police. And no other criminal than one acting under the orders of Tang-akhmut would dare to invade a building which so recently had been the scene of murderous activity. It would be, in their language, "hot."

No, there could be no doubt as to the identity of the trio. Whether they had trailed and identified Wentworth, he could not know. It was either that or some activity connected with the real motives behind the torture of the girl, Willa Abel….

Wentworth's own position was doubly dangerous, between the guns of the police and the agents of Tang-akhmut. He jerked his head sharply. No time to dwell on that. While a part of his brain kept watch, he must try to ferret out the answer to the question that had risen in his mind—the reason for Willa Abel's torture. Somewhere here there must be a clue to Tang-akhmut....

Wentworth smiled slightly, shook his head at the terrified woman, at Peck's darkly angry face. "I am alone, Peck. I always work alone... And I told the truth. *I have come to help you!* If you saw three men enter the building, they are probably the agents of the torturer, so we must talk fast."

Doubt crept into the detective's face. The girl, Clare, moved to his side, her hands groping for him while her eyes clung to Wentworth's. "Throw down that gun," Peck insisted stubbornly. "You can't escape from the building. If you are telling the truth about those other three men, they are trapped, too. We don't need help...."

Clare's hands gripped Peck's arm more tightly. "Wait," she whispered. "Wait...."

Wentworth bowed to her, "Thank you, Clare. You must answer a few questions for me. *Are you sure that Willa is dead?*"

Clare gasped. Her hands flew to her throat. "Oh, she is dead! Yes, yes, she is dead!"

Wentworth had been purely groping with that question. He had noticed from the newspaper accounts that no positive iden-tification had been made of the woman's body which had been strewn through the streets after the torture. At Clare's anxiety, his eyes narrowed a little. Clare was anxious either to believe, herself, that Willa was dead, or to have him believe in that death.

"I suggest to you," Wentworth said softly, "that Willa was taken away a captive by the torturers; that she is being held hostage...."

Clare took a staggering step toward him. "Oh, no! You don't know what you are saying...."

Wentworth's eyes were gentle. There was in his mind now no doubt that Willa was alive as he suggested, and being held hostage. It was a favorite subterfuge of Tang-akhmut, thus to enforce obedience. Clare twisted her white fingers together, swayed.

"In God's name," she whispered, "I have told you nothing! If *he* finds out..." Clare's curious emphasis on the "he" jerked Wentworth's attention wholly upon her. It could mean only one thing—that Tang-akhmut himself had presided over the torture of Willa Abel. But why? In Heaven's name, why had the torment of an insignificant clerk been so important that it had been almost Tang-akhmut's first act on reaching the city after his Sing Sing escape?

"PECK!" WENTWORTH cried softly. "Listen carefully, now! This man who directed the torture, Clare! This man whom you fear to have know that you have spoken! He is tall and high-shouldered and his face is thin and imperious, his nose like a hawk's. His eyes are yellow and they have a trick of widening like a cat's...."

Clare dropped to her knees, sobbing. "Oh, who are you?" she whispered. "Who are you that you know these things?"

But Wentworth's attention was upon Peck. He was flinging at him swiftly his reasons for believing that Tang-akhmut was

11

in Cincinnati, was directing the torture; citing the confirmation that Clare had given.

"The city must act at once and powerfully!" Wentworth cried. "Have you the strength and the influence to see to that?"

Peck was scanning Wentworth's disguised face intently with narrowed eyes. A flash that could be recognition widened them momentarily—and Wentworth remembered that three men of Tang-akhmut, as the girl had terribly confirmed they must be, were in the building! Almost, the intensity of concentration which had driven Clare to her revelations destroyed them all. But because Wentworth had trained himself through long years of constant living with peril, he heard the faint metallic rasp of the door's catch being released. With no more warning than that, Tang-akhmut struck!

Wentworth's marvelously trained reflexes flung him into instant action. At the first sound, he hurled himself toward Peck and the girl, knocking them to the floor. He sprawled on beyond them, gun in hand as he rolled to his back. He was barely in time. The door flung wide and, a sub-machine gun already speaking, three men sprang through. The Tommy gun's bullets flew wide at first. The shooting was intended to paralyze with fright until the muzzle could be pulled around to bear on the victims. Lead hammered across the wall, puffed plaster dust into the air, sent a mirror to the floor in fragments.

WENTWORTH FIRED deliberately the moment the operator of the machine gun was visible around the jamb of the door and his bullet flew true. The man whipped forward, bent double at the waist, took two staggering steps and went to his

knees. He stayed that way, forehead on the floor, body supported
by his murderous weapon.

Wentworth called out quickly,
"Stand steady, you two men—
unless you want to die, too!"

His two guns held firmly on
the other two hoods, armed only
with revolvers. Quickly they
lifted their hands, dropped their
weapons, and Wentworth eased to his feet. Peck scrambled up
and ran toward them. It had happened so quickly, the attack
and its ending. Wentworth could hear Clare's quick, sobbing
breath. He turned to her as Peck jerked down the men's wrists
and hooked them into handcuffs.

"You see," Wentworth said softly, "these men intended to kill
you. Tang-akhmut will not keep faith. You could help us and
you must—help us to find Willa…."

"No!" Clare gasped. "No, he would kill Willa!" She shook her
head pleadingly, eyes on Wentworth's face. "He'd kill Willa!"
FROM SOMEWHERE a strong rich voice echoed her
words harshly, a voice that Wentworth knew, which whirled
him in his tracks with a triumphant shout rising in his throat.
That voice was the voice of Tang-akhmut!

"Detective Peck," said the voice, "the man before you is Richard Wentworth, wanted for murder, charged with being the
Spider…."

Wentworth was already springing past Peck toward the hall-

13

way from which the voice seemed to speak. His guns were ready. If he could find and destroy Tang-akhmut… Blood pounded hotly to his brain… Peck ripped out an oath.

"By God, I knew your face was familiar!" He snatched for his gun, abandoned his prisoners. "Wentworth, you're under arrest…."

Peck dodged Wentworth's first blow, lifted his gun. And Wentworth was frantic with the need for haste. Somewhere here was Tang-akhmut… His fist shot through with vicious force and Peck collapsed to the floor. Wentworth could no longer hear the voice of Tang-akhmut, but dimly, it seemed to him, came the echoes of the Egyptian's mocking laughter. The two handcuffed gunmen were fleeing together down the steps, as if they obeyed orders. And Wentworth knew surely that it had been to accomplish their escape that Tang-akhmut had spoken. But there was the cordon of police about the building, of which Peck had spoken. Had that been a bluff? It must be so, since otherwise, the police already would be upon them, summoned by the blast of guns.

"Stop!" Wentworth shouted after the two fugitives. "Stop, or you are dead men!"

The gunmen were halfway down the flight of stairs to the floor below, but Wentworth pinned them with his gun muzzles. They saw that and jerked to a halt, hands lifted quakingly. They knew, as all the criminal world knew, the deadly accuracy of the Spider's guns. Tang-akhmut had done himself a two-edged service in naming his foe!

"Don't shoot, Spider," the men begged. "For God's sake, don't shoot!"

"Back up the stairs," Wentworth ordered quietly. "Move quickly!"

He was fighting blindly against Tang-akhmut. He could not know how next the Egyptian would strike, but it had seemed part of his plan that these two gunmen should escape. If he could thwart that... Wentworth was beginning to hope that the shots would not be reported to the police, but if they were, he must make sure that neither Clare nor Peck repeated Tank-akhmut's charge that he was the Spider. He must remain unhampered in his fight.

The cry of one of his prisoners, shrill and quavering with terror, struck dazzlingly across Wentworth's thoughts. The man pointed downward rigidly, cringed to the steps.

"Don't!" he cried. "For God's sake, not that...."

Something that glinted metallically flashed upward from the dimness of the lower hall, something that was sinuous and slender as a snake as it darted through the air. The screams of the two handcuffed men mingled. They crouched together, tried to dodge the glinting thing, but it moved too swiftly. And then it struck. Wentworth saw clearly what the weapon was in that moment, a long and slender cord weighted at each end. The middle portion of the cord struck the bodies of the two men, those ends whirled about them, wrapped them in a single, screaming bundle, and locked tightly.

It clung to the men and they stood rigidly, screaming. A moment their cries rose terribly, then they collapsed together on the steps, a limp—and Wentworth knew—lifeless huddle! Horribly, Tang-akhmut had repaid their failure!

AS THE two men screamed, Wentworth sprang down the steps. If Tang-akhmut hoped to intimidate him by the strangeness of his murder weapons, he was doomed to disappointment! Wentworth thrust one gun away as he raced downward, palmed the railing and sprang over it to the hallway below. Another of the slim, glittering cords writhed through the air toward him— too late. His timely leap had avoided it. Into the dimness of the hall, Wentworth's gun spat flame while his body was still in the air. The shock of his landing hurled him against the wall, but he rebounded and instantly was springing to the attack.

Somewhere ahead, a shrill laugh sounded. It was high and thin as a child's, yet it carried a cruelty and a mockery that no child could compass. Feet scampered away through the dimness as if a boy ran from the mischief he had contrived, but not quite like a boy at that. The weight on those feet was greater and there was a queer warped rhythm in their stride. Wentworth checked his mad pursuit and stood there in the darkness with a cold touch of dread tightening his scalp. The Spider was not a man to be racked by nameless fears, but there had been something horrible in that laughter, in the suggestion of those scampering feet that were childish and yet no child's.

Belatedly, he fumbled out a small flashlight and sent its concentrated beam ahead of him. Squarely across his path, tied from doorknob to newel post, was another of those deadly cords. In the direct ray of Wentworth's light, it scintillated with a thousand points of light and he saw that it consisted of a cord pierced by innumerable needles whose venomous points reached out thirstily in all directions. He did not need to examine the thing to know that those points had been dipped in deadly poison!

Furiously, Wentworth hurdled the murderous thing, pounded on down the hall. Four doors opened off it, and behind one of them he knew the creature of the shrill mocking laughter, the agent of this newest death weapon of Tang-akhmut, had disappeared. He bent, listening intently, to catch some hint of the fugitive's direction—and heard Clare's voice!

The sound came from above, broken, frantic with pleading. Wentworth could distinguish no words, but her tones were desperate. Damnation! The assassin could not have climbed the stairs in those few moments, unless... While Wentworth hesitated, torn between two quests, Clare screamed!

The Spider hurled himself at the stairway, sent a shot roaring ahead of him, hoping it might frighten Clare's assailants. God, the building must be alive with the agents of Tang-akhmut! Why none of them had shot him in the back, why indeed Tang-akhmut had bothered only to speak in the apartment instead of blasting Wentworth into death, as undoubtedly lay within his power, no man save Tang-akhmut could say. Perhaps he had feared to kill Peck and Clare. Perhaps he wanted them alive....

Fear for those two drove Wentworth to frantic speed. He hurdled the two dead gunmen on the steps, bounded to the door of the apartment. Locked! Furiously, Wentworth sent lead from an automatic into the lock, hammered with his shoulder. His first shot had killed all other sound. There were no more screams, not even Clare's pleading. The silence mocked the

17

Spider, goaded him… Then the door yielded and hurled him inward. He stood motionless for a moment in the drawing room, then raced frantically through the apartment, made a hurried search through the building. It was useless. Clare Hubbell and Adam Peck had disappeared. Wentworth's lips twisted bitterly. He had no doubt at all as to what had happened to those two. They were the captives of the merciless Tang-akhmut!

CHAPTER 3
THE HORDES OF
TANG-AKHMUT

ONCE MORE, with a swift thoroughness, Wentworth searched the apartment and this time, in a cubbyhole of an office he had mistaken for a closet, he found the crumpled body of a man. The man was middle-aged, his body thin but hearty. Glasses clung precariously, unbroken, to the bridge of his nose, and gray hair tufted above his ears. Plainly, this man was Dr. Zachary Abel whom Wentworth had come to question and succor.

As Wentworth lifted the man's limp body, he was conscious of a not-distant concussion, a muted explosion as if blasting operations were under way. The sound was followed in series by a half dozen other blasts, some nearer, some farther away. For a moment Wentworth stood irresolute, then he shook his head and moved expertly to revive Dr. Abel. Clare, in spite of her fears, had been tricked into making some minor revelations. Wasn't it possible that Dr. Abel, confronted with the knowledge that Tang-akhmut had struck at him a second time through his loved ones, would tell all that he knew? It was scarcely possible that the eccentric doctor could be the object of such concentrated attack without some hint of the motive behind the operations….

Despite his preoccupation with reviving the doctor, Wentworth's senses kept a keen lookout. He was convinced now that the entire foray had been planned to seize the detective and the girl, perhaps to kill the Spider also. Wentworth's dash up the stairs had left the way clear below and Tang-akhmut would not be slow to take advantage of it….

Wentworth exclaimed impatiently when he sought water to help revive Dr. Abel and only the hiss of air came from the opened faucet. He ranged through the apartment, opening other taps, but in each case the result was the same. No water was available. Strangely, the Spider's thoughts flashed to that series of explosions he had heard, and in that moment of pause, the hoarse, pulsing wait of fire sirens came to his ears. A cry rose in his throat. The water cut off and now fire had broken out. Was this some new machination of Tang-akhmut? Those explosions… Wentworth shook his head, frowning. Foolish to blame the city's every misfortune upon the Egyptian. He turned back to the doctor—and heard a machine gun. There was no possibility of mistaking the stammering death cough of that little weapon of murder! Without further hesitation, Wentworth hurled himself from the apartment.

For all his speed, Wentworth moved cautiously down the stairways, through the halls. Twice, he barely escaped death in cleverly set traps left behind by the minions of Tang-akhmut. The opening of a door dropped a writhing cord of poison needles almost upon him; as he strode along a hall, he felt the trip of a thread against his ankle and dived to the floor. Near him, something struck the wall with a dull concussion.

Instantly, Wentworth was up and running, breath caught in his throat No need to wonder about the weapon in that trap; he had heard the bursting of a gas bomb....

Out into the street Wentworth plunged at last, stood motionless, questing the avenue with swift eyes. The shriek of sirens was in the air again and there against the northern skyline mushroomed the black smoke of a widespread fire. The machine gun was silent, but in the street he saw the victims of its murderous fire. Three workmen lay upon their faces beside a crater in the pavement from which water gushed almost jubilantly. It made a low thick fountain there beside the bodies of the dead and where it washed across them, the water was tinged with red! Yet Wentworth had doubted the agency of Tang-akhmut in the cut-off of water. He knew now past any cavil that the explosions had all wrecked water mains; that the fires had been deliberately set—and that there was more to come.

THE RASP of running feet twitched Wentworth about to face the sound. A taxi had halted at the corner, blocked by the

RICHARD WENTWORTH

bursting flood of water, and down the pavement a man raced, long-legged. He ignored Wentworth, darted for the door of the apartment building. Wentworth's arm barred him.

"Don't go in there," he warned sharply. "Poison gas!"

The man bounced back from Wentworth's arm, his dark eyes wide and blank for a moment. They narrowed desperately. "But, man, the people must be warned!" he gasped to Wentworth.

The Spider shook his head. "No one in the building at all," he said quietly. "There's been a gun battle and everyone cleared out."

"Everyone," the man whispered, "then... then Clare...."

"Who are you?" Wentworth demanded sharply, "What do you know about Clare Hubbell?"

The man shook himself visibly out of his daze. "Clare Hubbell? I go to see her... But where is she, sir, do you know?"

Wentworth was studying the face of the man, keen, long-nosed, alert. He was bare-headed and his dark, careless hair laid a slab across a forehead that was high and pale. Wentworth told him quietly, "Clare Hubbell has been kidnapped by the torturers."

It was necessary then to give the thoroughly frightened man a brief story of what had occurred in the Abel apartment. Wentworth made it seem that he had been the companion of Detective Peck. He learned that the man to whom he talked was Hal Shields, a reporter on the *Times-Post*.

"Sent over to find out about the fire," he said finally. "I learned that there was no water, that the fires would probably get out of control and I hurried over to warn Clare. Damned funny thing, those water mains letting go...."

"Wait," Wentworth broke in shortly. "What banks or other storage places of wealth are in this district? What places that would be worth looting by the greatest criminal of our times?"

Hal Shields stared at Wentworth, then his eyes narrowed. "You mean the fires were set to give some crooks a chance to rob...."

"Quickly!" Wentworth interrupted. "First, what banks?"

Shields flung out his arms in a quick gesture. "The woods are full of them!" he cried. "We're right on the fringe of a financial district. That fire is only a half block from one of the biggest in the State, the Ohio Mechanics Trust. Then there's a national bank around the corner; and the American State...."

Wentworth pivoted and raced toward the taxi. "Come on," he ordered shortly. In the cab, he flung a swift direction at the driver, faced Shields. "You've got to get through to your paper with a warning of what threatens. It's not only the bursting of water mains, and fires; but the man behind these crimes has set killers to prevent any repairs from being made. Three workmen were killed in this very street! And you can say that police are sure the man behind these crimes is the Egyptian who escaped from Sing Sing death house, Tang-akhmut!"

Even in the rush of excitement, Wentworth was conscious that Shields' eyes were questioning him, probing into his features. If Shields were on the police beat, he would know most of the detectives in the city. He....

"You aren't a city dick," Shields said quietly. "I think you're a pretty wise hombre though, at that. Tang-akhmut, eh? What makes you so sure?"

A cold smile touched Wentworth's lips. His eyes bored for a moment into those of the reporter. "I heard his voice during the attack on Clare Hubbell's apartment," he said quietly.

"You know his voice!"

Wentworth nodded. "I helped send him to Sing Sing. I'm from New York, but there isn't time now to present credentials." His sarcasm was deliberately heavy. "Make the statement on your own responsibility if you like. My own presence here is being kept more or less secret. But I swear to you that Tang-akhmut is behind these crimes!"

Shields shuddered. "Good God, that beast! And Clare is in his power!"

THE TAXI whirled a corner and fell into the wake of an emergency repair wagon of the city's department of public service, whose siren sent the echoes ringing. Abruptly, Wentworth turned to Shields.

"Did Willa Abel work in the department of public service?" he demanded. "Did she have anything to do with the water department?"

"By God, she did!" Shields hurled back excitedly. "Something to do with keeping records on the water gates, taking readings, volumes… You know the sort of thing."

Wentworth realized that Willa Abel's information would be precisely what Tang-akhmut would have to possess in order to smash the water mains for any given area of the city! The scope of his discovery staggered even the Spider. Why, with such information at his finger tips, Tang-akhmut could destroy the entire city! Even without fire, the blasting of the water mains would soon throw the city into panic. Water available at every tap was a thing of which people thought little until the convenience was removed, but once that threat hung over them, they would

24

be in a panic The end of water supply meant also the end of sanitation. The sewers would dog and fester. Disease would spread....

"Guards must be set on all water mains!" Wentworth shouted to Shields, and explained the potential menace of Tang-akhmut's knowledge. "Tang-akhmut would not hesitate to destroy the city for his own selfish ends!"

He saw the incredulity in Shields' eyes. Ahead of them, the repair truck swerved and jerked broadside across the street. A half block away, a geyser from a busted main flooded the roadway from curb to curb. Instantly, men spilled from the truck. Two raced for a manhole at the corner, pried it up to get at the valve which would close the main, the water gate. Wentworth, who had leaped from the taxi, saw them bend together over the dark opening, heard their screams rise horribly. From the manhole flames blasted upward, blindingly white. The two men writhed briefly in the gutter, then were pitifully still. And the street split open. With a concussion that hurled Wentworth to the pavement, the water gate which alone could close the broken mains was blown up. A fresh and more powerful geyser of flame was followed by a sustained gush of water.

Grimly, Wentworth pushed to his feet. He knew with a dreadful certainty that every attempt at repair would be met with some such horror as this. He found the foreman of the repair truck and shouted the warning in his ears, ordered him to report to headquarters and spread there, too, the warning that murder waited for the repairmen, that they must have police guards. Shields he urged to the same task.

"What are you going to do?" Shields demanded.

Wentworth jerked his head. "I'm going to guard as many of those banks as I can. Make that part of your warning, too, and get police here quickly! Tang-akhmut is out to make a killing!" He smiled thinly at the mockery of his words. Shields' white face twitched in answer, then he looped about and ran wildly back along the street.

Wentworth loped lightly in the opposite direction, toward the banks. His reloaded guns were snug against his sides in their holsters and now and again as he ran, eyes questioning sharply over the streets, his fingers touched the butts briefly. The scent and the smarting sting of smoke was thick in the air; the reek of chemicals. Chemicals would be the fire department's sole hope of checking the blaze and Wentworth knew their supply would be inadequate. The only recourse then would be dynamite… They would hesitate to use that.

GUARDS STOOD outside the Ohio Trust as Wentworth hurried past, posted beside the door with drawn guns. Their eyes were anxiously on the thick smoke that smeared across the sky. As he neared the second bank on his self-appointed rounds, Wentworth realized that he was too late. Tang-akhmut already had been at work here! Men in bank guards' uniforms lay dead upon the steps, one with the glittering death cord of Tang-akhmut about his throat! Wentworth sprang to the door, and the interior was a shambles, but deserted. Those who lay upon the floor might have seen the looting, but they would never speak of it, never speak of anything again.

Back to the street Wentworth pelted, his eyes questing to the first bank he had passed. Less than a block away and around a corner, it stood. With a grim tightening of his lips, Wentworth strode back. It was curious that those armed guards at the door had not heard the shots that had slain so many in a brother institution. It was queer that if they heard, they only stared at the smoke streaking the sky... Openly, the Spider mounted the steps toward the bank's doors. The eyes of the two guard and their guns swiveled toward him.

"No dice, buddy," one of them growled. "This bank is closed until the fires over!"

If Wentworth needed confirmation after the bank guard's words, he received it in that moment. From the depths of the bank came a scream. It poured wide open from a man's throat, without form, without words, a cry of mortal anguish, the eyes of the two men in guard uniforms flew to each other.

"You take him," one said shortly to the other.

Wentworth laughed, and the sound of it was eager and glad. At last he was at grips with the men of Tang-akhmut! He sprang lightly sideways toward the guard who had directed his companion to shoot. Wentworth's hands moved almost delicately to the gun butts beneath his arms. His twin automatics blasted together!

The Spider never struck at innocents, nor at the defenders of the law, but these men had already twice condemned themselves; first as allies of Tang-akhmut; second with the determination to kill Wentworth because he had heard that tortured scream from within. They were doomed and they died with that single blast of Wentworth's guns. The same leap that had carried the Spider toward one of the pair of false guards carried him on toward the doorway. He was through the great main portals of the bank before his shots had ceased to echo.

Instantly, his eyes took in the full picture of the interior; the parallel counters of the tellers' windows to each side, the

entrance to the vault at the rear. Stretched on the floor were the customers who had been so unfortunate as to enter the bank. The robbers had not bothered to take them prisoner, but had blasted them into instant death. The workers had been treated similarly, but some of them had managed to swing shut the great door of the vault. The scream of the tortured man rang out again from behind one of the counters and Wentworth spotted the robber guards.

There were four of them, one at each corner of the counters, crouched behind their protection with ready sub-machine guns resting before them on the marble tops. Wentworth fired once before he lunged head-foremost to the floor, and that shot hurled the nearest machine gunner backward, head wrenched backward from the impact of forty-five caliber lead. He died without a sound—then the two other guns that could bear on Wentworth burst into action.

If he had remained stationary or merely sought cover in those first violent moments of action, the Spider would have died within seconds. He did neither. That dive to the floor was only the initiation of his attack. Striking on a shoulder, he rolled swiftly toward the counter whose guard he had slain. Nor were his guns idle. He could not hope for accurate shooting but he fanned the counter behind which the nearest machine gunner crouched. He powdered marble dust into the man's face, sent deadly lead skipping within inches of his body. That and his swift movement gave him the brief respite he needed. He got his feet together under him, dived head first over the counter and somersaulted to his feet. He had a full two-fifths of a second to steady himself while the machine gunner at the other end of the counter brought his weapon to bear. That was more, much more than the Spider needed. His bullet drilled the killer squarely between the eyes.

THE SCREAMS of the tortured man had ceased and the

excited cries of the robbers flew back and forth. Wentworth, crouched behind the counter, calmly reloaded his automatics and holstered them. He caught up the machine gun of the first man he had killed and began the second phase of his attack. The killers undoubtedly were experienced in the use of their weapons, but now they were up against a master, a man who had made a study of firearms and their expert use a fetish. While the spraying bullets of the two machine gunners still on their feet scored on the marble counter and lifted toward their target, the Spider fired two deliberate bursts. These other fools depended on the panic which the mere thought of machine guns usually induced in their prey to hold him motionless until their questing bullets lined up the target. Wentworth's bursts went straight to their marks—and the two machine gunners were hammered into bloody death.

What followed was a hopelessly one-sided battle, though it was one man against a half dozen. The killers of Tang-akhmut had no defense against the accuracy of Wentworth's gun fire. His flat laughter mocked and unnerved them.

"The Spider has come for you, fools!" Wentworth derided them. "The Spider brings you death!"

Five more men fell before the Spider's deadly gunfire, a sixth Wentworth allowed to escape to carry to his master the news of defeat. Swiftly then, Wentworth hurried over the bank, seeking someone whom he might help. It was useless. Those who had survived the first burning blast of criminal gunfire had been executed one by one with "mercy shots" through the head. Nor had the tortured man, his body horribly mutilated, been left alive. In all the vast silence of that bank, there was only death.

Anger burned hotly through Wentworth's veins. So much of this slaughter had been useless, even from Tang-akhmut's viewpoint. The damnable Egyptian was intent upon his reign of terror; torture and wholesale murder... Wentworth's lips shrank back coldly against his teeth. By the gods, there should be a reckoning! His hand went to his vest pocket and withdrew a slender cigarette lighter of platinum. He thumbed its base and stooped above the bandits he had slain—and when he passed, there gleamed on the forehead of each the Spider's challenge to a Tang-akhmut, a scarlet symbol in rich vermilion that claimed these dead as the Spider's own, *the seal of the Spider!*

As he straightened after that grim task, Wentworth heard a footstep lightly at the door. He whirled, gun in hand, and his fierce gaze stabbed into that of the reporter, Hal Shields. Shields' face was deathly pale. He came forward and his feet made awkward fumbling of his steps. He wet his lips before he could speak.

"The Spider!" he whispered. "You are... the Spider!"

Wentworth thrust his automatic away, smiled slightly. There was still the fierceness of battle within him. A man did not fight death, fight the enemies of mankind and slay, without emotion. But his voice was quiet.

"Yes, the Spider," he said. "I prevented the looting of this hank. I was too late to save the people. And there is no time to delay. There may be still other robberies in which Tang-akhmut has been delayed...."

A strong shudder seized Shields. He pivoted stiffly on his heel and walked with Wentworth to the street "I saw the bank guards," he said heavily. "One of them was Sparks Hutton, a local crook."

"Affiliated with any gang?" Wentworth asked swiftly.

Shields nodded. Words seemed laborious in his throat. "Been working with Maddern— Fritz Maddern," he mumbled.

The shaking of the ground beneath them almost threw Wentworth to the pavement. He caught hold of Shields, felt the jar and gush of a heavy explosion.

"Dynamiting buildings to stop the fire," Shields said.

THEY PASSED a second and a third bank that had been looted. In the fourth, police were already at work. The streets were beginning to fill with people. Wentworth saw two boys get down on their knees and drink the flood of water in the gutters. A woman filled a big kettle and went stolidly back into the house. All very well for the present, but the great main water gates would be closed soon and the district would be utterly deprived of water. The city would have to transport drinking supplies, but there would remain the menace of disease....

Wentworth saw these things with half his mind while he

canvassed the battle that lay ahead. He had won a minor victory over Tang-akhmut in preventing the looting of that one bank, but it was not by such petty tactics that he would triumph. It was plain that the Egyptian was uniting local crooks under his leadership, throwing his terrible weapons into the hands of criminals. The Spider could intimidate such men as this Fritz Maddern, perhaps delay their alliance with Tang-akhmut until other measures could be taken to find and destroy the Egyptian.

If only he were not stripped of all help in his fight with Tang-akhmut! But the Egyptian had seen to that. It had been part of his earliest strategy to make Wentworth a fugitive, stripped of position and wealth. Doubtless he had known enough of Wentworth to realize that, in such a position, he would not permit his usual helpers to risk an association which might land them in prison. But if only Nita van Sloan—

Resolutely then, Wentworth pulled his thoughts away from the one woman in the world who had his confidence and his love. Nita van Sloan was in New York, still hoping to hear from him. She would know when she read of the day's events where he was. God knew he could use her counsel at such a time; could use her keen brain for the work with which he must entrust Shields if it were not to interfere with his own operations against Tang-akhmut. He smiled drily to himself. He thought he could depend on the reporter for this much, especially since it would mean big news for his paper… Wentworth began to talk rapidly to Shields.

"I'll pay Fritz Maddern a visit," he said, "but meantime there is a way in which you can help. In his foray on New York, Tang-

akhmut had assumed another man's identity. On several occa-
sions, he caused the prosecuting attorney, Oscar Dodgington,
to fall into a hypnotic coma and usurped his personality. In this
way, Tang-akhmut built up a scapegoat for his crimes and only at
the last minute did I uncover his plan and forestall it. It is likely
Tang-akhmut will install himself similarly here in Cincinnati
and I want you to canvass the list of possible men—they would
be wealthy or at least prominent—whose place Tang-akhmut
might conceivably take. Try to discover anything peculiar in
their recent behavior or health. It is even likely that they might
be the victims or enforced observers of some of the tortures...."

"Not much to work on," Shields said keenly, "but I see what
you're driving at! Listen, Spider, I'm all for you. I know you killed
some men back there, but you had to save the bank! And I think
you've done some swell work lots of times. I read every line I can
get about you. If there's anything at all I can do...."

Wentworth's hand closed on the reporter's shoulder. "I appre-
ciate that," he said gently. "You just work along the fines I've
mentioned. If I find anything pointing to any one man I'll
communicate with you. And if I can find Clare...."

Shield's hand clasped his warmly; then the reporter was
gone. Wentworth peered about him with anxious eyes. The
police apparently had taken full charge of the banks now and
there was little more the Spider could do on the scene of Tang-
akhmut's crimes. A call on Fritz Maddern now might catch him
unprepared... Grimly, Wentworth turned away. It would be
the Spider who called on Maddern, the hunched and be-caped
figure that criminals everywhere feared terribly. A visit to his

hotel room first to get the materials of disguise....

All about him in the streets, Wentworth saw the evidences of Tang-akhmut's raids. Not only were banks strewn with dead men, but the promise of trouble to come was in the faces of the people who wandered numbly about the streets. Already stores that sold soft drinks were besieged by the thirsty. In the oppressive city heat, their supplies would soon be exhausted. And afterward... Wentworth shook his head sharply. Before there could be any recurrence of the disaster of today, the Spider must strike surely and finally!

At the hotel, he took an elevator directly to his floor, hurried toward his room. Strange that he should think now of Nita van Sloan. If only he dared communicate with her... His footsteps beat a muffled rhythm along the carpeted hall and, dimly, he heard a woman scream.

"Police trap, Dick!" the woman cried. "Run for your life!"

Instantly the door of Wentworth's room was whipped open. Instinctively he dived to the right toward the stairs that wound downward. His stabbing hand caught the iron newel post as he went past. It wrenched his shoulder, but jerked him to a halt, whipped him down on his knees behind that slight barrier. In the same instant, guns began to blast!

CHAPTER 4
TANG-AKHMUT STRIKES BACK

WENTWORTH HAD a glimpse of a half dozen men crowded together in the doorway of his room shooting at him, heard shoots below and the heavy pound of feet coming toward him up the lower flights of steps. He had recognized the voice that cried out to him though it had shocked his heart. Nita! Nita Van Sloan! But how on earth? He had not thought that the one person in the world who had clung to him through his downfall was within a thousand miles of this hotel. It was plain that she had been taken prisoner and held in his room; that somehow she had recognized his footstep and cried her warning even in deadly peril. Wentworth felt his heart lift at the thought of Nita....

But even with her help, he seemed doomed. The police, without challenge, had opened a deadly fire that kept him nailed to the spot. And more men were charging from below... Well Wentworth knew that he had Tang-akhmut to thank for this betrayal. The man must have had him trailed from the moment his plane landed! And he had plotted cleverly.

If the men who opposed him had been criminals, Wentworth would have shot it out with them without compunction. The Spider's deadly fire would soon, have carved a passageway to safety. But the Spider, however much he might step outside the law, never made war with its representatives. Rather than shoot at the police, he would himself be killed!

The issue was not so simple as that. He had read something

else from the fact that the police fired without challenge. Was not that very circumstantial proof that the police authorities were subject to Tang-akhmut? Wentworth allowed a brief, bitter smile to cross his lips. He was exaggerating, surely. The police were too afraid of the Spider to take any chances. That was all. They owed no allegiance to Tang-akhmut. It made no difference at this particular moment. All that mattered was that they were bent on his destruction—and he could not fire back.

Wentworth cast about him for some chance to escape. The elevator shaft was not ten feet behind him, but its door was closed. Diagonally across the hall was the entrance to another room. If he could reach that doorway... He shook his head. To cross that corridor amid all this buzzing lead meant certain death. His eyes quested down the stairway. On the platform, halfway to the floor below, was a window which opened on a five escape, partly open. Wentworth's hopes began to revive.

But to reach that window he must stop the police fire for a few seconds. Otherwise, he would offer them too fine a target. Feverishly, he sought a way... A fire hose was looped against a valve at the platform, but that was too slow. What then... A ghost of a smile touched Wentworth's lips. Supplementing the hose on each floor was a large fire extinguisher of the old-fashioned type, a copper tank that held five gallons of sodium bicarbonate. At its top was a small vial of sulfuric acid. To use the extinguisher, you turned it upside down and allowed the acid to flow into the bicarbonate. It discharged a frothy liquid in a stream that would carry for fifty feet.

The moment Wentworth's eyes lit on the extinguishers, he

was in action. A single shot at the one above, opposite the door from which the police fired; a second shot at the one on the floor below. His shots were carefully placed, drilling squarely through the vials of sulfuric acid within. Instantly, the frothy chemical spewed from the bullet holes! A second shot ripped open the side nearest the police and they were deluged with the stuff. It was harmless enough, but its effect was startling.

Before they had recovered from their surprise, before the police below could do more than hurl a few startled bullets through the blinding froth, Wentworth was down the stairs and had ducked out the window onto the fire escape. As he passed the fire hose, he twisted the valve wide open and the water ripped the hose from its support, sent a high pressure stream playing indiscriminately over the stairs.

OUTSIDE THE window, Wentworth raced upward. He had chosen his room carefully and he knew that another fire escape on the opposite side of the building went down past his window. It required a space of moments to reach the roof, to cross to the opposite side and start down the fire escape again. The police would not be far behind him for the hose and the fire extinguishers could cause only a momentary delay. Throughout the building, he could hear excited outcry. The guns of the police banged futilely. They shouted instructions at each other, but none of them was in sight. Wentworth moved cautiously down the second fire escape toward his room, peered cautiously in. A policeman stood guard over Nita, but he was staring into the hallway rather than at her. Nita herself was handcuffed to the foot of the bed on which she was seated.

Wentworth did not attempt to open the window. Despite the noise, it would undoubtedly be heard and the guard warned. He smashed the pane in with his elbow and went through in the same movement. The policeman spun toward him, but too late.

Wentworth's fist went cleanly to his jaw and the man bounced off the foot of the bed and hit the floor flat on his back.

After her first start of joyous surprise, Nita sat quietly waiting. She only whispered, "Dick!"

Instantly, Wentworth was on his knees beside the policeman. The man's handcuffs were missing, so Wentworth was sure he had the key to those that held Nita prisoner. He found it, freed Nita and hustled her toward the window, arm tightening about her waist. He laughed softly as he handed her over the sill.

"Nita, darling, you saved my life again!" he said. "How is it that you always manage to arrive just in time?"

Nita was hurrying down the steps of the fire escape toward the floor below. She tilted up her chin to smile at Wentworth. "It might be," she called back softly, "because I love you, because I know when danger is near you!"

He helped her into a room two floors below. A man was sleeping drunkenly in the bed, newspapers sprawled over the floor. He did not stir.

"Into that closet," Wentworth ordered Nita quietly.

He sprang to the telephone. "What time is it?" he demanded, and when the operator told him, he exclaimed angrily: "I left a call far one o'clock. Why wasn't I called? I suppose the telephone doesn't work either? Suppose you test the bell. Yes, that's what I said. Ring it long and loud!"

Wentworth hung up and darted to the closet, closed the door gently and stood waiting, an arm again about Nita's waist. The telephone bell rang, rang, and rang again. The sleeping man stirred faintly, sat bolt upright and lifted the receiver. He said, grumpily, "Sure it rang. What the hell do you think?"

He was sitting there on the side of the bed staring at nothing when the police knocked on the door. He slumped over to it, staggered back as a cop bounded in.

"Anybody come through your room?" the officer demanded.

The drunk stared at him, then cursed. "You got the hell of a nerve crashing into anybody's room like this! What the hell do you mean?"

The cop swore, whirled and bounded out of the room again. The drunk shut the door and grumbled some more. He went over to the bathroom and the shower began to hiss. Quickly Nita and Wentworth left the room and slipped back into Wentworth's quarters. They had already been thoroughly searched, so the two would be safe there. For safety, they hid in one of the two closets in the room, talked in whispers.

WENTWORTH'S ARMS closed about her and his lips found hers in the darkness. She knew it was for her sake that he sought to bar her from his dangerous work. Her mere presence with him was an acknowledgment that she knew his "sins" and condoned them. It made her an accomplice of Richard Wentworth, wanted for murder!

"But how did you find me, dear?" he asked.

Nita shrugged. "I knew from the newspaper stories that Tang-akhmut must be out here. I knew you'd come here. And,

Dick, it's a bad thing for a man in your position to form fixed habits. Do you know that three times before when you were in Cincinnati you stopped at this same hotel?"

Wentworth laughed. "I'm glad you're not on the other side, Nita. You know too much about me. Tang-akhmut undoubtedly followed me from the moment I landed—or else the police are in his hands."

"They recognized me when I went to the desk downstairs," Nita said soberly "and brought me to your room. I didn't learn anything from their conversations except that they were going to open fire the moment they set eyes on you. Oh, Dick, if I hadn't followed you, if I hadn't recognized your footstep in the hall…."

But Nita's presence here was madness. She had been arrested as a precaution by the police but if she continued at his side, there would be much more serious charges against her.

It was fortunate that Nita could not see his face in the darkness. Wentworth had long schooled himself to impassivity, but with Nita his guard was down. His face hardened. This was madness. Until they were clear of the hotel, they were in peril. Not that escape from this one trap would set them free, but at least the danger would be less imminent… The door of his room was not watched, but Wentworth knew that every exit of the hotel would be closely guarded—unless the police were convinced he was already out of the building. He pressed the signal button of the service elevator, which was used by hotel employees. He pretended surprise when the operator told him that. He laughed, "Well, take us down anyway. We don't want to wait for the other cage."

The Negro porter smiled and Wentworth and Nita descended in what they hoped would be an unwatched shaft.

"Quite a racket around here this afternoon," Wentworth said conversationally to the porter.

The porter agreed. "Ah thought those cops would never stop hunting that Spider fellow. They been over the whole building and keep watching and watching. There's one downstairs comes up with a drawed gun every time I open the door. He shore got me nervous."

"I can imagine." Wentworth glanced at Nita and saw that her face was taut and white. "They ought to be more careful with those guns. Where is he? I don't want the lady to run into anything like that!"

The porter wagged his head. "For a fact, it's skeery." He giggled. "S'pos'n I take you down to the basement. He'll think somethin's up and duck down there. Then we'll come right back up to the first floor."

They did that and heard the policeman shout as they kept on down to the basement. As his feet thudded down the stairs, the elevator slid back up again. Wentworth gave the porter a five dollar bill from his scanty score as they stepped out. Wentworth heard the Negro's voice call softly after him.

"Good luck, Spider man!"

Nita's startled eyes flashed to Wentworth's but they did not speak until they were in a taxi which they directed to the Union Depot.

Wentworth smiled a little wistfully. "One man, at least, who likes the Spider," he said. "How much easier my work would be if more people understood that I am working for them, if they would help me instead of trying to run me down." He shrugged, squeezed Nita's hand. "The help came very opportunely at any rate."

AT THE Union Depot they walked through and got a taxi on its far side. Wentworth rapidly outlined his plans for paying a visit to Fritz Maddern.

"It's pretty obvious that Tang-akhmut intends to unite the most powerful criminal elements of the city," he said quietly, "and continue with his looting. If he destroys the city in the process, it will trouble him not at all. Once let him get his organization firmly established and well financed, and nothing can stop him. He can sweep the nation!"

Nita's hand closed on his arm. "I am going with you to this interview with Maddern," she said firmly. "I can keep watch outside, make sure that you aren't surprised by the police. If anything happens, I can take a hand."

Wentworth turned to protest, but the steady directness of her violet eyes told him how useless was protest. He laughed softly. "Now I can conquer anything," he whispered. "With you by my side...."

The cab drew to a halt a block from the apartment building which Shields had named as Fritz Maddern's headquarters. Nita and Wentworth strolled casually toward it... And flames burst from the concrete pavement. It was incredible, yet there, within a yard on all sides, the dazzling white fire which earlier Wentworth had seen kill two water repairmen was leaping up from the concrete as high and higher than his own head! The thing came without any warning at all and, within seconds, the weakness of the heat was upon him.

He gasped for breath while all about him the crackle of these phantom-like flames roared. He tried to protect Nita from the fierceness of the heat, got a gun in his hand. He could see nothing except the phantom-light of the flame. Futile to attempt to smash through that superheated barrier—better to wait until they faded. That was it... Wait until they faded. Wentworth crouched to the pavement and held Nita close. It seemed to him that there was an overpowering perfume in the air, a cloying sweetness. His throat closed. Shouting, Wentworth forced himself to his feet. He began to hurl lead out into the circle beyond the flame, at shrill laughing figures he could not see... These were the agents, the weapons of Tang-akhmut! Good God, had Shields betrayed him? Shields had known he was coming to see Maddern.

Wentworth fought against the increasing disconnectedness of his thoughts. He was on his knees; his gun was empty, and that scent which clogged his nostrils—Gas... As he slipped into impenetrable darkness, Wentworth saw in his mind's eyes the arrogant face of Tang-akhmut with its hawk-like lines, and its eyes that were like the unwinking, tawny eyes of a great cat!

CHAPTER 5
THE POWER OF PHARAOH

THE FIRST vision Wentworth beheld on reviving, as his prescience had shown him in his last moment of consciousness, was the tawny eyes of Tang-akhmut. Mocking, they gazed deeply into his own and instantly Wentworth was aware of struggle within him, of the deep resistance of his will. Before this he had fought the hypnotic power of Tang-akhmut, and he knew its strength. He pulled his eyes away, pushed up dizzily from the carpeted floor on which he lay. Tang-akhmut allowed the grim thin line of his mouth to relax.

"You are too clever for me, Wentworth," he whispered. "Much too clever! I had thought that if I caught you in the first, moment of consciousness, I might gain hypnotic ascendancy over that stubborn will of yours!"

There was mockery in his voice and as always, Wentworth felt the cold fury of anger rise within him. This calm, intelligent man had directed the maniacal murders that had terrorized Cincinnati; this man had smashed the city's water mains and killed dozens of people in his robberies of the banks merely to augment the established terror. But he could be cool and mocking with his prisoners, catlike....

Wentworth forced himself to smile through the cold hatred that gripped him, forced himself to gaze calmly about the chamber in which he found himself. A high-ceilinged room, it was hung with silks until it seemed a desert tent. Almost beside him lay Nita, her breathing deep but irregular. He leaned toward her, but there was no symptom of returning consciousness! A tautness crept aver him. The cold gaze of Tang-akhmut bored into his back.

"She revived some time ago, Wentworth," the Egyptian said

"Look behind you, Wentworth! Look at Nita before you strike!"

softly. "Her present sleep is hypnosis. Her will is not so great as yours!"

A cold fear for Nita stirred deep within Wentworth, but he hid it, pushed himself steadily to his feet. There were no guards in sight. To all intents and purposes, he was alone with Tang-akhmut! His hopes lifted, but he realized their futility. He was unarmed. Before he could kill Tang-akhmut with his bare hands, as he mightily longed to do, a dozen men could reach him.

Tang-akhmut smiled. "You have quite properly figured the possibilities, Wentworth," he said. "You have no chance of killing me! And here is an added deterrent. If I die, Nita dies also! She is subject to my will, and I have willed it so!"

Wentworth's faculties were dulled from the effects of the gas he had inhaled. His brain struggled with Tang-akhmut's statement. Queer, occult things had come out of the East before this, but was Tang-akhmut's claim a possibility? He thrust the thought aside. Regardless of the means employed, he and Nita were doomed, unless… but what hope was there?

SOMETHING VERY like a shudder touched Wentworth then. He felt strangely helpless, stripped of power—and that was not his normal reaction to difficulty. There was something so monstrous about this calmly feral Oriental! Wentworth consciously braced his will. He must work for time, time to discover his situation, to plan… He thrust his hands deep into his pockets and found a ray of hope in the fact that one secret at least had not been penetrated. There in the lining of each pocket were still two tiny tools, one a keen blade which would sever bonds; the other a minute length of spring steel with which he could pick locks, spring handcuffs… He hid the spark of elation that began to burn in his breast.

"You're probably lying," he said carelessly to Tang-akhmut "There is a will to self-preservation in all of us which would prevent your fulfilling that threat upon Nita. It does not matter. In the end, Tang-akhmut, I shall defeat you! In the end I shall kill you!"

Something that was almost admiration made a gleam in the tawny cat eyes that never blinked from their regard of Wentworth. "I am glad, very glad that my weaklings did not kill you, Wentworth," he murmured. "With you destroyed, life would lose some of its zest! There are so few really resolute enemies!" He leaned forward a little; his right hand stroked the arm of his chair. "I have devised a little test for your resolution, my enemy!"

The stroking of his hand coincided with a soft, distant ringing of chimes, obviously a signal, for the curtains of heavy silk were whipped aside by two giant Negroes, naked to the waist, each of whom carried a bared scimitar in his right hand.

Through the opening, a queenly woman moved with indolent pace, a lovely creature in the shimmering transparency of her draped robes; robes that floated behind so that their ends seemed to evanesce into the air. Her hair was richly auburn, bound by golden fillets that united to form a rearing hooded cobra's head above her calm brows, the crown of the two Niles. Wentworth knew her. Once he had held her yielding in his arms, and once she had tortured him almost to the point of death! It was the sister of Tang-akhmut, Issoris.

Tang-akhmut spoke to her with the mockery that never

seemed to leave his sonorous voice. "A pair of lovers, Issoris. I thought you might care to see them!"

Issoris turned her head with a slow stateliness, then her eyes fell on Wentworth and a tautness raced over her body. It was no less lovely, but its majesty now was the majesty of a stalking lioness. The breath hissed between her white, even teeth. Her black brows drew down into a straight line.

She snatched a dagger from her sash, crouched forward. Within a pace of Wentworth she paused, reached out the slim blade toward Wentworth's breast. Then she smiled with a crooked writhing of her full lips. Wentworth's eyes held hers quietly.

"No, that would be quick and I do not wish it to be quick," Issoris laughed caressingly. "And first we must play a while with this love of yours! Ho, brother!" She turned to the throne. "Ho, brother, summon slaves to bring the rubber wands!"

Wentworth saw the shudder that swept over the Negro slaves at her words. They knew what the rubber wands meant, and Wentworth himself knew only too well. They could flay the skin from a human body! Wentworth saw that Issoris still gripped the dagger tightly in her fist and on the instant he acted. In a bound he had the weapon. He flung her aside, sprang to the throne. A fiery exultation was in his breast. Here was a weapon that could kill quickly. He lifted it—and Tang-akhmut did not move!

He spoke calmly, "Look behind you, Wentworth! Look at Nita before you strike!"

WENTWORTH SUSPECTED trickery, but he could

not be sure. He sprang past Tang-akhmut, whirled and put the knife point against the Pharaoh's throat! Good God! Nita had a knife, too, he saw with staring eyes. With her own hand she pressed a dagger against her throat in exactly the

same manner Wentworth pressed the blade against the carotid artery of the Egyptian!

"Thrust if you wish, Wentworth," said Tang-akhmut, "and see your loved one die!"

"Nita!" Wentworth cried. But he knew it was useless. This man's will spoke to Nita. Perhaps he had primed her for precisely this scene, coached her with words before he had recovered consciousness. How else had the knife been placed in Nita's hand? He had summoned Issoris with the sure knowledge that she would draw her dagger. God, the effrontery of the man, the cold courage. Wentworth's lips drew thin. Even if it cost Nita's life… Arms seized him from behind, wrenched the dagger from his hand. There were a half dozen of those brown arms about him and he was helpless. He saw that Nita's hand, gripping the knife, was still poised above her throat.

"It's all right, Nita," said Tang-akhmut. "You may put your knife down."

Wentworth was dragged backward and gyves were fastened about his ankles. His wrists were locked together behind him, chained to the wall, and he felt the cold stone of the wall press against his back. Nita lay supine on the floor. Issoris was on her knees before her brother's throne. "Brother, I ask thee one boon, only one! Let me have the man and woman—and *the rubber wands!*"

Tang-akhmut rose slowly from his throne and stepped down beside Issoris, drew her to her feet. There was an enigmatic smile on his lips as he glanced toward Wentworth, toward Nita. He led Issoris toward the yellow curtains, bent to whisper in her ear. As he whispered, Issoris began to laugh. She threw back her head and laughed until the room rang with it, until the husky beauty of her voice became cracked and harsh. Even after she had passed through the curtains, Wentworth could still hear her laughter echo. The sound of it slowly tautened his muscles, brought coldness to his heart. When a cruel woman laughed....

They were alone in the draped hall now, Wentworth and Tang-akhmut and the sleeping Nita. Tang-akhmut crossed slowly until he stood before Wentworth.

"Three times today I have tried to kill you," he said pleasantly, "and each time you have escaped, either through the cowardice of the assassins or your own intelligence. It is only added proof that I need you in my work! Do not let us quibble over terms. I hold your life and that of your woman in my hands. To such a colleague as you I would not be a stingy master!"

Wentworth met his gaze calmly, feeling the beat of the Pharaoh's mighty will. There was no attempt at hypnosis now, but there was a cold menace. Wentworth felt it tangibly—and he could not get the laughter of Issoris out of his thoughts. It would be foolish to say that Wentworth felt no fear. His was the truer courage which recognizes fear and scorns it. His face was scornful, drawn rigid by his hatred of this man. Yet he spoke quietly.

"Tang-akhmut," he said, "you should know the futility of such a proposition, or of trying to coerce me into alliance with crime. Criminals greater than you have tried to force me to obey by threatening the woman I love. What I told them, what I tell you now, is not an empty boast. I will not yield. I will repay any injury to Nita a hundred-fold!" He paused. He had to fight to keep his hatred from strangling him. "In the end, *I shall kill you!*"

On Tang-akhmut's lips his thin smile played again. "Yet I shall compel you, Wentworth. I need your brain. You shall obey me!" His eyes did not leave Wentworth's. He called, "Nita, arise and come to me."

LIKE A sleep-walker, Nita arose and crossed the room. When she stood beside him, Tang-akhmut ordered, without emphasis, "Nita, cut off the little finger of your left hand."

Nita lifted her left hand and set the blade of the knife against the base of the finger. She moved the knife and a little thread of blood ran down over the whiteness of her hand. Wentworth's jaw set rigidly. He knew that perspiration beaded his forehead. If only his manacled hands could reach Tang-akhmut's throat. If only he could reach that lock pick which the chains and his clothing kept from his hands. Resolutely, he kept his eyes on Nita's slowly moving hands, saw the dagger edge bite a little more deeply into the flesh. He was aware of Tang-akhmut's gaze, yet Wentworth would not speak. He would not. If he allowed Tang-akhmut to move him with this minor torture, the man's feral cruelty would know no human bounds... Tang-akhmut spoke quietly and Nita desisted. Her hands dropped to her sides and the thread of blood ran down her little finger and dripped, dripped to the floor. Her eyes looked through Wentworth and beyond him.

"I have no wish to maim her!" Tang-akhmut said, his voice almost caressing. "So much beauty is given to so few of her kind!" His long-fingered hand lifted to Nita's shoulder, closed, possessively. "Do you wish other demonstrations of my ability to coerce you, Wentworth?"

Wentworth gazed on Nita's unmoved face, at her wounded hand. What this man commanded, she would do. She was under the full hypnotic sway of his will. Whatever he commanded... There was a swollen, aching thing where Wentworth's heart should be and its every beat shook him, strangled him. God, that Nita should suffer so for her love of him! But he could not yield. It was not only a matter of personal integrity. If he submitted to this man, there was no one to fight him. The police were efficient in their way, but with this madman's genius... Wentworth forced his words out between his teeth and his voice held the ring of tempered steel.

"I will not yield, Tang-akhmut. In the end, I shall kill you!"

Tang-akhmut made a movement of sharp impatience with his hands, his eyes flamed dangerously. "You fool!" he said harshly. "Men do not defy me and live!" Wentworth met his gaze unflinchingly. He had his manacled hands against the cloth of his coat now, feeling for that sliver of sharp steel which was hidden in its lining. If he could force that through the cloth....

Tang-akhmut's lips pulled back from his long, narrow teeth.

He nodded slowly. "I like the stubbornness of your will, Wentworth, but I cannot permit defiance." He turned to Nita, hand on her shoulder again, and his grimace became a smiling cruelty. "Such men as you love deeply, Wentworth. Observe…" He said slowly to the unmoving girl beside him. "Nita, dear, I am your lover, Richard Wentworth."

Animation came to Nita's face. A smile ineffably tender curved her lips and her hands lifted to the shoulders of Tang-akhmut, her lips lifted.

"Your lover greets you, Nita," Tang-akhmut murmured, and bent over her.

Wentworth tasted blood and realized his teeth had ground through his lip. Nita's hand had made a trail of blood across Tang-akhmut's shoulder and he fixed his eyes on that. His gaze became hard and narrowed. Through the cloth his fingers had found the sliver of steel. He worked at it… God, *Nita*.…

Nita flinched away from Tang-akhmut's caress. "Dick!" she whispered, her eyes on the Egyptian's face. Then she laughed a little shakily. "How shocking of you, Dick!" She went back into the arms of Tang-akhmut, her face lifted, hungry for caresses.

"Nita!" Wentworth said sharply, urgently. "Nita, that man has tricked you. Nita, look into my eyes."

Under the touch of Tang-akhmut's hands, Nita stiffened a little, but did not turn toward Wentworth. Instead, it was the mocking cat-orbs of the Egyptian which swung in his direction. If only he could hold the man in parley for a while, he might free his hands. His ankles would still be secured, but once let him get his hands on the man's throat—He remembered the tracery

55

of blood that Nita's hands had left. Why… she had dropped the knife. It must be there under the feet of Tang-akhmut.

WENTWORTH BUNCHED his shoulder muscles hard, swelled forward against his gyves so that Tang-akhmut could not see the small movements as he worked the bit of steel through the lining of his coat….

"Tang-akhmut," he said deeply. "Don't you realize that you are destroying the last shred of chance that I might serve you? Even if I could compromise with my honor, I could not suppress the hatred that you are creating. The thing you are doing…."

Tang-akhmut said slowly, "Your hatred does not concern me. I have ways to guard myself against it. But I demand now your unequivocal oath to serve me faithfully. I know your reputation, Wentworth. You will not belie your word!"

The sliver of steel cut through and found the flesh of Wentworth's fingers. He joyed in the pain of it. Now he must twist his wrists so that the sliver could reach the lock, manipulate the bolt….

"Modify your oath, Tang-akhmut!" he urged hoarsely. "Do not demand the impossible of me!"

Tang-akhmut laughed, looked down at the swooning face of Nita. "Swear or not as you like," he said. "I am not sure that this woman is not worth more to me than you. You have truly exquisite taste, Wentworth."

"Modify your oath, Tang-akhmut," Wentworth repeated.

Tang-akhmut lifted his head and for a cold instant Wentworth was sure that he suspected what went on there behind Wentworth's back. But Tang-akhmut only waited to smile… "I will not modify *my* commands," he said. "For the rest, I still have ways to coerce you." His voice softened, became a murmur as he drew Nita closer into his arms.

"It is our wedding night, beloved," he whispered. "A while ago when the preacher married us, he made me the happiest of men. Are you happy, dear?"

And Nita's arms tightened about Tang-akhmut. Her voice was a paean, "So happy, lover!"

"We have waited so long, Nita, dearest," whispered Tank-akhmut. He led her across the thick-carpeted floor to the divan and Nita sank upon it, that smile of tenderness still upon her lips. Tang-akhmut stood gazing mockingly across the chamber at Wentworth, then he, too, sank upon the divan. His long-fingered hands....

Wentworth hurled furious words at Tang-akhmut while his own hands worked feverishly. After seeming years, one cuff fell from his wrist. It was easier then to work on the second. Both his hands must be free from the chain that held him against the wall. His ankles were secured, but there on the floor before him was Nita's knife. He could reach that by dropping on his knees. A single swift throw then....

"What a small man you are, Tang-akhmut!" he cried to the Egyptian, "that you must usurp another man's place to trick a woman! I thought that even the dogs of the East had more honor. And lacking honor, too much pride to have to trick a woman into love...."

Tang-akhmut snarled angrily. He thrust up from the divan.

"Fool, do you think Tang-akhmut has any need for such as her? Or that I need to masquerade in your place."

Wentworth laughed wildly. Both his hands were free, the gyves hung against the wall and the knife was there on the floor. Let him but fall upon his knees and snatch it... But first Nita must be restored to her own will....

"A very small man, Tang-akhmut," Wentworth taunted. "Restore Nita and see how little her master you are! You can so easily hypnotize her again—after you have failed!"

Tang-akhmut fought down his anger, laughed once. He turned to the couch. "I bid you awake, Nita, when I give the word. Awake and remember the caresses I have given you and their author! Nita, awake...."

Nita stirred languidly and on the moment Wentworth acted. He slipped to his knees and there was almost a sob in his throat as he snatched up the dagger. His voice rolled across the chamber: *"Tang-akhmut, I shall kill you!"* With a low cry, the Egyptian whirled about and Wentworth whipped his knife hand forward, threw the dagger in a glittering line of light straight for the breast of Tang-akhmut!

CHAPTER 6
SHRILL LAUGHTER

WENTWORTH DID not wait to see the effect of his throw. If it failed for any reason, he must be ready to press the battle to its very end. A strong exultation raced through him. He snatched at the gyves on his ankles, set swiftly to work with the lock-pick.

"Nita!" he cried. "Nita, kill Tang-akhmut!"

He felt the lock-pick catch on the lock of one anklet, and while he manipulated it he threw a swift glance toward Tang-akhmut. Tang-akhmut's face was twisted in pain and rage. His left forearm was transfixed by Wentworth's hard-thrown knife and Nita had seized him from behind, trying to strangle him with locked wrists. Wentworth closed his lips firmly on the curse that beat against them. He could not waste breath... The lock of the second gyve. His hands flashed in their work. Damnable to have Tang-akhmut escape him by so narrow a margin as a fore-arm interposed between knife and heart. At last the second lock rasped free and in the same instant Wentworth was bounding across the room—He checked, eyes darting about the chamber. Except for himself, it was empty!

In those few fleet seconds Tang-akhmut and Nita had disap-peared!

A thin, shrill laughter rang through the room, laughter that jerked Wentworth's mind back instantly to the battle on the darkened stairway beside Zachary Abel's apartment. The laugh-ter that had accompanied assassinations performed with the cords of poisoned needles. His head whipped toward the sound, toward the cobra-entwined throne....

From behind the throne leaped the travesty of a man, a hunchbacked thing with a misshapen head, no taller than an eight-year-old boy! The creature's body was nearly full-sized, but his arms and legs were ridiculously small. It was a dwarf of

59

such hideous mien that Wentworth felt almost nauseated at sight of him.

The dwarf jerked a whip from a leather case across his shoulders and the whip writhed and glittered. With a shout, Wentworth flung to the attack. For he recognized the whip! It was the same material as those deadly cords, laced through with hundreds of poison needles!

Even as Wentworth raced forward, a second and a third dwarf, a whole troupe of hideously malformed men poured from the shadows, some with poisoned bolas or whips, some with lashes of leather. And while Wentworth was still yards from his goal, the lights went out!

Panting for breath, Wentworth hurled himself toward the drape-covered doorway. Long practice had enabled him to retain his sense of direction in the dark and it served him in good stead now. He burst from pitch darkness into a hallway, and seized a scimitar from a wall hanging.

Darkness crashed down in the hallway and the patter of feet raced away. Wentworth stood still, swaying, the scimitar groping out into the blackness. He brushed aside draperies at his side, moved along behind them until he found a door. He went through that and a dim light showed somewhere ahead. He went toward it, found a room into which daylight poured.

Wentworth's breath panted from him sobbingly. Dimly he could hear the shouting and the pounding of pursuit. He stared out of the window and saw a wall-enclosed garden just beneath. There was another wing of the building that jutted out at right angles and Wentworth could see three stories rising above the

Tang-akhmut's dwarfs were masters of cruelty.

one in which he stood. Quickly he made his decision. He drove the hilt of the scimitar through the glass.

"Nita!" he shouted. "Nita, where are you?"

He knew that he betrayed his whereabouts by that cry, but he was past caring. If he could find and rescue Nita… If he could only reach her and they could fight side by side. He peered and shouted again, and high up, on the top floor of the wing, he saw a bit of white flutter at a window. Once, twice, three times, it waved, then it was yanked back from his sight. With a great cry, Wentworth finished the smashing of the window. He gripped the scimitar's keen blade in his teeth and stepped out on the window sill.

AT THE corner of the building there was a drain pipe from the roof. Wentworth sprang to the ground, reached the drain pipe in leaping bounds and swarmed up it with feet braced against the two walls at the corner. He was opposite the second floor when a man dashed out into the garden and opened fire with the revolver.

Wentworth dangled by one hand and whipped the scimitar from his teeth. When the man got set to fire again, Wentworth threw. The man dodged, but he had misjudged the force and speed of the throw. The whirling blade caught his shoulder and the base of the throat and buried itself. Wentworth climbed on.

In another few moments of frantic effort he grasped the edge of the roof. It was a Mansard type, very close to perpendicular for more than the height of a man, after which it sloped almost flatly to the peak. There were dormer windows at short intervals in this outer slope and it was from the farthest of these that a signal had answered his cry for Nita. Up the nearest dormer Wentworth climbed, and raced along the flat top.

"Open the window wide, Nita!" he cried.

He darted to the far side of the dormer, dangled down the steep slope in its protection. He heard the men shouting, running to get a clear shot at him. He groped for the window one-handed, found it and made a swift grab with his other hand. He missed his hold. His body swung out over the edge and dangled stories above death. Bullets pinged into the slate, crunched into the woodwork beside his hand. Then a woman's hands grasped his from within. It was a struggle, the ultimate drain on his strength to inch head first over the sill, but he achieved it. He strained his eyes against the dimness of the room. Nita? Why was she not in his arms?

"Nita!" he cried urgently. "Nita, where are you?"

"In God's name, Spider, save me," a woman's voice whispered. "Tonight, Tang-akhmut will give me to the dwarfs!" And it was not the voice of Nita!

Wentworth stared, his eyes becoming adjusted to the dimmer light, and despair seized him. He had taken this desperate chance to save Nita and he had climbed into the prison room of—Clare Hubbell!

CHAPTER 7
A DESPERATE CHANCE

L OOKING AT Clare Hubbell, Wentworth knew that the girl had deliberately led him to think Nita was trapped in this room. She had been willing that Nita remain a captive so that she herself would escape. Contempt rose in Wentworth. He turned his back on the girl and strode to the window.

"Do you know where Nita is held prisoner?" Wentworth demanded harshly.

"Oh, God, no," she whispered. "I don't know. I haven't seen her! Oh, please, hurry, hurry. In a few moments it will be too late."

The rush of feet in the outer hall confirmed her warning. Bullets continued to thud through the window and a fine snow of plaster dust sifted down over Wentworth, whitening the floor.

He strode to the door and wheeled a bureau in front of it, braced a chair under a drawer and wedged a leg into a wide crack in the floor. The floor was old, made of foot-wide boards, and the shrinking of the wood had left great gaps between them. He wrenched a leg from a chair and used it as a lever. If he could take up a part of the floor… An axe was hacking at the barricaded door; the treble rage of the dwarfs rose shrilly.

Finally Wentworth raised an end of a board. Clare seized it with her hands and strained upward, too. Within a few minutes, two of the boards had been taken up and there was nothing between them and the freedom of the room below save thin laths and plaster. An axe split through the door panel and a revolver cracked. The bullet went wide but the barricade could hold out only seconds longer. No time to hack at the laths. Wentworth caught up the broken chair and smashed it downward without result.

"Follow me!" he snapped to Clare. He climbed on a table,

jumped high and came down feet-first on the lath and plaster barrier! It smashed and Wentworth plunged through to the floor below. Splinters gashed his legs and body, scraped across his face. He struck the floor below heavily, rolled aside.

Wentworth bounded instantly to his feet, peering about the room into which he had dropped. It was empty save for himself, its furnishings coated deep with dust. In three strides, Wentworth was at the door, listening. He heard the thud of Clare's drop into the room even above the racket of the attack on the barricade. That noise would help to cover their movements for a while. Thank God this door was unlocked... He slipped out into the hall and, with Clare on his heels, stole toward the stairs whose banister he could see dimly.

ABOVE HIM there was a final crash, then a loud outcry. The gibberish of the dwarfs wailed and from the garden Tang-akhmut's deep voice answered. Wentworth whirled down the stairs, Clare's heels beating a swift tattoo in his wake.

He bounded across the hallway of the third floor, listened an instant at a doorway before he whipped into the room behind it. Then he crouched with Clare while the pursuit clamored through the halls. When there was a brief respite he hurried toward the wing where he had battled Tang-akhmut. Clare's sobbing breath was at his elbow and impatience stirred in him. Anything he accomplished must be done with absolute stealth and Clare was a hindrance. Yet he could not send her back into captivity. Regardless of her behavior, she did not deserve the fate that would be meted out to her ultimately by Tang-akhmut. But no more did Nita! Wentworth's fists clenched hard at his sides.

NITA VAN SLOAN

He strode on resolutely, but more carefully. He was painfully aware of his many small wounds, of weakness.

All about them the shouting continued; footsteps raced back and forth. Twice Wentworth was forced to hide in fortunately empty rooms while dwarfs raced past like a hunting pack. Finally he reached a right-angle turn in the corridor that marked its juncture with that of the other wing. The dwarfs had gone that way only moments before. Peering around the corner, Wentworth found himself gazing directly into the eyes of a giant Negro, who held a bared scimitar in hand!

Unhesitatingly, Wentworth sprang to the attack. His fist cracked to the man's jaw, but his strength was diminished. The man reeled, then swayed forward, the scimitar rising for a death stroke. Wentworth kicked the Negro's shin savagely, seized the scimitar and struck with swift necessity. Behind him, Clare uttered a choked cry as the Negro shivered out his life upon the floor.

Wentworth ignored her. He was alive with hope. He sprang to the door which the Negro had guarded, found it locked, and used the perfect steel of the scimitar as a lever. The lock burst and Wentworth stormed into the room, stood stock-still. The perfume of Nita's presence was all about him, but Nita herself was gone! Wentworth laughed exultantly. She would return!

He darted out of the door, seized the body of the Negro and dragged it into the room. Then he saw the blood… It could be

washed up, but there was no time, no time. Wentworth crouched inside the door, scimitar in hand. If he were quick enough… Clare shivered and made little moaning sounds.

Impatiently, Wentworth warned her to silence. His keen ears caught the clatter of approaching footsteps and he was warily alert. The sound drew near—and a dwarf cried out. With a curse of disappointment, Wentworth hurled himself into the hallway, scimitar raised above his head. He had a blurred impression of a half dozen men there. A dwarf's poison whip flicked at him, but the steel blade severed it, slithered on in a thrust that sliced through flesh. The dwarf screamed terribly as Wentworth bounded around the corner.

"Flee for your life, Dick!" Wentworth heard Nita's voice call to him steadily. She was behind a rank of a half dozen men, three of whom bore guns. The others were whip-armed dwarfs. Even as Wentworth lunged to meet them, a dwarf sprang forward and hurled one of the deadly cords at him. Wentworth dropped under it, sprang up and struck. He was among Nita's escort in a flash, the sword a flail of death.

Two more of the men fell before his attack, but the gunmen thrust Nita savagely through a doorway and sprang after her. The door slammed in Wentworth's face. Bullets crashed through the wood within inches of his head.

A sob of despair tore at Wentworth's throat. The echoes of the shots would bring a stream of fighting men. He could hear the swift pound of their feet, their triumphant shouts. More bullets poured through the door.

"You can't help me, Dick!" Nita's voice came muffled through the panel. "Hurry, Dick. Hurry. I'm all right. Tang-akhmut won't harm me *unless you are present to see!*"

WENTWORTH HAD stooped and recovered a poisoned bolas that missed him, gripping it by the harmless guard in its middle. What Nita said was true, he recognized, but it was bitter to come so close, yet fail. Tang-akhmut's very cruelty would dictate that he wait until Wentworth was present to torture Nita… Within moments, Wentworth knew he would be overwhelmed, but right now he could still escape, summon the police….

"You're right, Nita!" he cried. "I'll be back!"

Bullets swerved toward the sound of his voice, but he bounded to the angle of the hallway, the bolas swinging above his head. He whirled the corner and there was a compact group of men charging him. Neither dwarfs nor Negroes, these men were obviously drafted from the city's Underworld. Tang-akhmut had warriors of all kinds, alike only in their deadliness. The guns of the men blazed the instant they spotted him, but they were terrified by that whirling bolas. Those in front slid to a halt, tangled with those behind them. Wentworth let the poisoned thing fly and his assailants were too crowded to dodge. They shouted and the bolas caught one man on the throat. Its deadly ends flailed back and lashed two others behind him. Then Wentworth was upon them with the scimitar. The fight was brief and bloody. At its end, Wentworth snatched a gun from the floor where one of the men had dropped it, and fled. Clare now ducked out of hiding and followed.

Hatred of the girl burgeoned in Wentworth's heart. He

reasoned against it, but the emotion remained. It should be Nita who ran beside him to freedom!

Swiftly, he coursed the halls, turned finally to the garden wall. Bullets still screamed after him, but he boosted Clare to the wall's top, used her slender arms as a rope for his own ascent. The girl whimpered with the strain upon her shoulders. Bullets burned the brick dust into her face. At last Wentworth was over the wall and they fled into the woods which pressed close.

In a covert, safe for the moment, Wentworth turned to Clare.

"I am going to destroy Tang-akhmut's fortress here," he said swiftly, "but we must have help.

"You must find your way to a road and get a ride to the nearest town. People generally don't know about Tang-akhmut, so your story is that Nita has been kidnapped and that the kidnappers are holed up here! Say that you were kidnapped, too, and escaped; that more kidnappings are planned…."

Clare started and caught Wentworth's arm. "That's true," she whispered. "Tang-akhmut is going to kidnap more people! There's a big dance in Cincinnati tonight; the season's debutantes will all be there, the richest families in the city. Millions of dollars. Tang-akhmut is going to kidnap them all tonight, and—" Clare shuddered—"I don't know how he is going to do it, but he plans to get the fathers here, and… and give me to the dwarfs. With that threat about what he will do to their daughters if they don't pay up, he thinks he won't have any trouble collecting! He told me all that!" She bowed her head and sobbed. "Oh, Spider, I know I was a coward to wave to you when you called to Nita, but when he told me about those horrid little dwarfs...."

Wentworth stared past the girl blankly. The plan that Tang-akhmut had outlined was incredibly bold, but for that very reason it had excellent chances of success. He gripped Clare's arm, glanced at the declining sun.

"This makes it even more important that you get away at once," he said harshly. "It must be well on toward eight o'clock now! Tang-akhmut may strike at any time after the debutante ball starts... I'll go for help, too, in another direction. Get to a telephone also and warn them in Cincinnati!"

With the urgency of a city's need upon him, Wentworth crept off through the woods.

CHAPTER 8
TANG-AKHMUT'S REVENGE

PRESENTLY, WENTWORTH struck a narrow, winding road and, a few moments later, the sound of a racing automobile engine came to his ears. Flourishing his captured revolver, he flagged down the car and commandeered it from its startled driver, sped forward.

Wentworth lifted his eyes to the light glow of Cincinnati on the northern horizon. How remote it seemed! But never too remote to escape the long arm of Tang-akhmut! Wentworth dared to jerk his eyes from the road and discovered a radio in the car as he had hoped. It was vital that he learn what had happened in the city during his absence of twenty-four hours. There was almost always a news broadcast at some point on the dial....

The announcer's voice came vibrantly to his ears... "The city owes an undying debt of gratitude to these two brave men, Detective Adam Peck, and Reporter Hal Shields. Few men would dare as they have dared to denounce the united Underworld under the leadership of that arch-criminal of all times, the Spider!"

Wentworth started, stared at the radio. Was it possible that he had heard aright? He listened intently and slowly his mouth grew hard, his eyes became glittering points of light. Shields and Peck had united in a damnable lie. They told in the columns of the *Times-Post*, said the announcer, how Peck had been captured by a band of criminals who still held his fiancée captive. While there he had overheard a deal in which the Spider, for a split of the profits, promised to plan the crimes for a group of criminals which had organized the entire Underworld of Cincinnati!

Wentworth shook his head dazedly. In God's name, what reason could Peck have for manufacturing such a lie? How had he escaped Tang-akhmut? The manner of his escape was recounted by the announcer, but it was ridiculous to believe that Tang-akhmut, or Tang-akhmut's men, would have been as careless as this indicated. Slowly, then, Wentworth began to realize the true situation. Peck had been a captive of Tang-akhmut, and subject to the hypnotic will of Tang-akhmut. He probably believed the full truth of the thing he had told! This was the deal into which Tang-akhmut had tried to drive Wentworth, which he had resisted at such fearful cost to Nita and to himself. And the Egyptian had struck viciously in reply!

How would the police heed now a warning from the Spider? How could he pound through their skulls the fact that Peck had only fancied he had heard such a deal while under hypnotic influence? The police probably would not even believe hypnotic influence was possible! Yet Wentworth must accomplish all that before he could warn the police and put them on guard against the kidnapping of the girls whom Tang-akhmut had marked this night for doom. Otherwise, the police would think the warning part of some subtle criminal plan....

GRIMLY, WENTWORTH realized that though he might phone his warning to Cincinnati, violently though he might long to remain behind and assist in the attack on Tang-akhmut's fortress and so rescue Nita, only one course remained open to him—The Spider must speed to Cincinnati. In person he could accomplish what a thousand phone messages would fail to do. He could avert this new catastrophe threatened by Tang-akhmut. It was not alone the kidnapping for ransom of those girls. It was not alone the fact that undoubtedly scores of persons would be killed by Tang-akhmut's cohorts during the raid. But through the kidnapping, Tang-akhmut would gain control over many of the wealthiest families of the nation.

On and on ran the tale of death and violence, all laid at the door of men who operated under the Spider's banner. It was mad, but how could the people doubt Peck and Shields? Shields and Dr. Zachary Abel united in accusing Wentworth of partici-pating in the torture of Willa.

73

A town, a cluster of lights, an echoing roar from building walls, flashed past Wentworth. He braked violently and hunted a telephone. He was damnably conspicuous with his torn and stained clothing, but it could not be helped… With his tale of kidnapping, his whisper that he was one of the gang who had been double crossed, Wentworth had little difficulty in arousing the local police to call in State troopers to strike at the fortress in the woods. Wentworth was forced, when the call was finished, to dash on to another town before phoning Cincinnati lest the local officers run him down by tracing the call.

WENTWORTH HESITATED over his call to the Cincinnati police to warn them of Tang-akhmut's plans. If he made the call anonymous, it was doubtful if the police would act upon it. If he revealed his identity… The "double crossed member of the gang" story might cause them to throw a weak guard about the ball, but that would be useless. Nothing less than the full co-operation of the police could possibly hope to cope with Tang-akhmut. It was far from certain that even then he could be beaten….

Finally, Wentworth determined to call the head of the bureau of detectives. Captain Lacost, Wentworth recalled, was his name, and he had a reputation for belligerence and honesty. The Spider could not determine in advance what course to pursue with Lacost, but such a man was infinitely less likely to have fallen subservient to the graft that Tang-akhmut would be sure to disburse than would be his superiors… Captain Lacost's voice came briskly over the wire.

The butler and the maid were unconscious on the floor.

Wentworth spoke quietly and swiftly, warned the captain of what threatened at the debutante's ball.

"No one on earth would try to get away with a thing like that," Lacost shouted. "I haven't got time to talk to cranks!"

"Wait!" Wentworth's voice rang with quiet authority. "The man who is planning the raid is Tang-akhmut. Ask Adam Peck about him! Force him to tell you! Wait, damn you! I will tell you who I am. I am the Spider!"

Lacost's voice rose excitedly over the wire. "You damned crook!"

Wentworth smiled twistedly. "I am coming to Cincinnati to prevent the raid on the ball if I can," he said slowly. "If I find that you have failed to take the proper precautions, the wrath of the Spider will descend upon you! Look up my record. You will learn whether it is the Spider's custom to ally himself with crooks! You will learn he keeps his word. Act—or die!"

Wentworth started the car swiftly forward on the road to Cincinnati and realized that the momentary delay had now stripped him of the excitement which had borne him up previously. He was once more bone-tired. On his swift way northward, Wentworth munched at some chocolate bars he had bought in the little shop from which he had phoned. They helped to restore him somewhat… He fully realized that he had betrayed himself by the call. He had told Lacost that he was the Spider, that he was on his way to Cincinnati. Lacost then need only find from what source the phone call had come and throng the road between that point and Cincinnati with officers! But it had been necessary. It meant only a longer delay in reaching the city.

Wentworth swung into a cross-road and raced for some other highway which would parallel the one he followed. It offered no guarantee of safety, of course, but perhaps some expedient would present itself, an airplane—It took an hour to discover a flying field, the low, long line of an airplane hangar with its wind-sock swinging fitfully against the glow of the northern sky.

Wentworth was low in funds as always since he had been stripped of his wealth by Tang-akhmut. He must either persuade the caretaker to turn over a plane to him or take it at the point of his gun! But there was no time to consider such matters. He jerked the car from the road and halted in the shadow of the hangar. It took time to arouse the man who kept watch, and more time to convince him—even with a revolver—that he must unlock the hangar doors and turn over the plane.

Finally, the plane motor was warming and Wentworth bound the watchman to his cot. He took the man's clothing to replace his own, cleaned up and disguised himself as best he could while the engine warmed. "You'll be glad when you read the papers tomorrow that you did this," he told the man. "I am the Spider, and...."

"You crook!" the man swore at him. "Hooking up with crooks! Helping to kill and rob honest folks! Damn you, I'd like to...."
WENTWORTH MOVED heavily back to the idling plane. Tang-akhmut had struck a bitter blow when he had released Adam Peck to spread the word that the Spider was his

ally... Into the cockpit Wentworth climbed, sent the ship scudding into the sky.

He would reach Cincinnati no more swiftly by the plane flight, he realized, for he must land on the outskirts of the city. He had no way of telling how much time had sped, but it must be close to eleven o'clock. Surely Tang-akhmut would not delay much after that. Within fifteen minutes, Wentworth was hovering low over the city toward where Eden Park lay. It was on a hillside, its lawns on many different levels, but the wide straight roadway just inside the Gilbert Avenue gates might be long enough. He had no choice....

Twice he swooped over the stretch he had chosen and each time a car blocked his way. They scuttled for cover on the third circling, however, and he threw the plane steeply toward the pavement, fish-tailed to reduce speed and set the plane down exactly in the middle of the thoroughfare. A car loomed ahead, whirling through the broad gates, skidded to a frantic halt at sight of the plane. When Wentworth finally stopped his machine the propeller was within two feet of the car's radiator.

Instantly, Wentworth sprang to the ground, ran toward the car. "It's a matter of life and death!" he shouted at the driver. "Get me downtown fast!"

The young man driving had a girl beside him and was reluctant, but Wentworth gave him no chance to demur. He shoved him aside from the wheel, whirled the car in a tight U and burned down the steep slope of Gilbert Avenue. There was a frown of concentration between his eyes. If the police refused to take his warning seriously, or refused to help, what course was open to him? What could he do single-handed against the forces of Tang-akhmut?

The man and woman whose car he was driving asked eager questions, but he told them nothing. What could he tell them—that single-handed, he was going to battle the army of Tang-akhmut?

He hit Vine Street and raced toward Fourth where, at the Sinton, the debutante ball was being held. A block from the hotel he dropped from the car. The man shouted after him, but he caught no words. He must be in time! Nearing the main doorway of the hotel, he slowed to a walk, and gladness touched his heart. Those three men who scanned him alertly as he went past were plainly police. His warning had been heeded!

Wentworth contrived to get together a small make-up kit at a corner drug store and, with this, he went into a late restaurant and retired to the wash room. When he emerged a few moments later he had made certain basic changes in the lines of his face. His nose had been broadened with putty until it's intelligent, thin bridge was gone; his eyes pulled hypocritically down at the outer corners and his mouth was twisted into a sneer. There was a trace of belligerence in his stride, in the twisting movements of his head as he looked about him. He went to the side door of the Sinton and no one attempted to prevent his entrance, though several men eyed him closely and one unobtrusively followed. WENTWORTH FROWNED, studying the police precautions. The lobby was virtually filled with guards and the hallways to other doors were watched. When Wentworth started up the stairs toward the ball room, a politely insistent man stopped him.

"I want to speak to Captain Lacost," Wentworth told him quietly. "I have some information for him."

The man gestured Wentworth to follow and went swiftly to a small room off the balcony at whose door two uniformed policemen stood. Inside, Captain Lacost was ensconced behind a small desk. He was talking into the telephone when Wentworth entered. Lacost finished, looked up sharply. He had wide-spaced gray eyes, a long jaw.

"Well?" he rapped out.

Wentworth made his voice harsh and nasal. "A fellow landed a plane in Eden Park," he said, "and grabbed hold of my car, made me bring him down here. He gave me five bucks to bring you a message."

The captain eyed Wentworth alertly, hands pressed down on the desk. "I got a report of the plane," he growled. "What's the message?"

Wentworth pretended skepticism. "This guy in the plane claims he's the Spider. He says to tell you to get your men some gas masks."

The captain had thumped to his feet. "Where is this Spider?"

"He skipped out up the street," Wentworth told him. "I think he came in the hotel. He kept asking questions about what it was like inside. But I ain't never been inside the Sinton before." Wentworth stared around him curiously.

The captain continued to eye him. "Describe the Spider," he ordered.

80

Wentworth gave a faithful if somewhat sketchy description of himself. "Geez, ain't you going to do what the Spider said," he demanded. "That guy is smart. He said make your men wear gas masks. He didn't say what for."

Captain Lacost glared. "Take this egg outside and hold him." He caught up his phone and shouted orders to search the building for the Spider, to have gas masks handy. Wentworth had a reason for telling the police he thought the Spider was in the building. If they searched it thoroughly, they might uncover the men of Tang-akhmut! And it occurred to him that an anesthetic gas would be the perfect means to affect the kidnapping of the debutantes.

Under guard on the balcony, Wentworth kept a keen watch on the lobby below. He saw that the police were vanishing one by one, to return with some bulky object, clearly the gas masks, under their coats. The music of the dance floated to him and he located the double French doors that opened into the ballroom. A severe faced butler was taking invitations from a few late arrivals. Within, there was a whirl of men's formal black and the gay dresses of the debutantes. Wentworth frowned. Whatever the police did, they could not prevent the gassing of that entire assemblage, if such happened to be Tang-akhmut's plan. The intended victims would be helpless throughout the battle to come....

"Say," he urged his guard, "how about giving me one of them gas masks? I was in the War and I know what gas can do to a fellow."

The policeman hesitated, then called a curt order to one of

the uniformed men at the captain's door. Wentworth inspected the mask with business-like efficiency, nodded and dangled the thing from his belt. He was counting on Tang-akhmut to use a gas whose odor gave warning, but he had no guarantee that such would be the case. In dangerous mines, they used mice or canaries to detect the gases which always menaced the workers. But there was no time to persuade the police to that.

PEERING DOWN the lobby, Wentworth saw a petite maid start across the lobby with a Pekingese on a leash. The dog moved placidly ahead at first, then abruptly paused, lifted its nose and sniffed, ran back against the legs of the maid, reared up and yapped excitedly. Wentworth's mouth set grimly. He was guessing, of course….

"Gas!" he shouted. *"Gas!* Put on your masks!" There was authority in his voice. Without hesitation, the men on guard drew on their masks, as did Wentworth. The captain bolted from his office.

"Who gave that alarm!" he demanded. "Who did it, I say?"

His voice died. He lifted an uncertain hand to his head. Wentworth leaped to him and whipped the mask over his face, sprang back to the railing. The Pekingese which had given the alarm lay unconscious on its side. As Wentworth looked, the maid wavered and plunged forward on her face, unconscious. The butler at the ballroom door was braced against the wall, clutching his throat. All over the lobby, masked men held guns in their hands… Tang-akhmut had begun his attack!

The waiting, the tenseness of the men, dragged on in silence. At Wentworth's side, Captain Lacost slowly recovered his strength. He put a hand on Wentworth's shoulder, thanking him silently for the help with the mask.

Wentworth nodded toward the doors where the butler had fallen, and strode that way. The captain followed, motioning men immediately around him to close in. The music had faltered to a dismal end. On the dance floor, couples were staggering weakly toward the windows. Many already had slumped to the floor in pitiful little heaps. Here, Wentworth knew, was the major danger point. He stepped full into the hall and stood on guard. If he could open the windows… He hurried along the wall, and abruptly dizziness seized him. The devil—could the gas penetrate his mask? Holding his breath, Wentworth ran for the window, caught up a chair and smashed the glass to fragments.

At that precise moment, he heard a woman scream terribly, heard the anxious shout of a man. A red flickering light danced over the street, and up the stone wall toward the window Wentworth had burst open ran a hot tongue of flame! From behind him, he heard a muffled cry and moments later, the shout of "Fire! Fire!" was echoing. Wentworth had anticipated one of Tang-akhmut's stratagems, but this other, more horrible threat, he could not have guessed. The flames were spreading with incredible rapidity and two hundred and fifty of the city's youth lay unconscious, starkly helpless, in their path!

As the thought of turning in an alarm crossed Wentworth's mind; the sirens of fire trucks rang through the night. But they were far away, and the fire spread so quickly. Wentworth whirled to summon the police who wore gas masks—and the door was blocked by their collapsed bodies! Merciful God, what could he do alone? Wentworth raced for a fire hose, jerked it loose and—nothing happened. There was no water! A savage curse tore at Wentworth's throat. Tang-akhmut had burst the water mains, too! God, he must find a fire extinguisher. If he could protect them until outside help arrived....

Dizziness seized Wentworth. He staggered, dropped to his knees. He had forgotten the gas! Only the fact that he had smashed a nearby window had saved him thus far. Furiously, he ripped the mask from his head, held his breath while he smashed window after window with a chair he caught up. He gasped, reeled dizzily, but clung to his senses. Then he hunted for an extinguisher to turn at the fire, fought on in a daze in which fire, smoke and the inert bodies on the floor whirled crazily about him.

When firemen trooped into the room and sprang to attack the flames with hand extinguishers Wentworth could only sag against the wall. Slowly, he battled back to full possession of his faculties. His body still weak, he watched unconscious men and women carried out. The firemen fought the flames as if they knew their tasks. Could they be the operatives of Tang-akhmut? Wentworth thrust the thought from him. No, the prompt arrival of the fire equipment which was filling the streets had prevented Tang-akhmut from finishing the raid he had so efficiently begun. If they only kept vigilance for a while longer... Wentworth staggered against the wall and braced himself there, fumbled along it toward the unconscious police. He must have a gun, in case....

HE CAUGHT up two long-barreled revolvers from among

the unconscious police, thrust them into his belt, reeled out into the hall. Smoke and red flames were creeping along the corridor without hindrance. The lobby was filled with rain-coated firemen who dragged the unconscious to safety but little was being done against the flames. Wentworth fired a shot high over their heads.

"Get chemicals in here!" he shouted. "Be quick about it!"

One of the firemen whipped out a revolver and fired at Wentworth! The bullet fanned his face and as he dodged back the fire-weakened railing gave way under his hand. He flung prone and threw lead over the heads of the men, stopped that with a groan. They might be kidnapping some of those they carried out, but at least they were rescuing men and women from the course of the flames!

There was a quick step behind him. Wentworth rolled over, guns ready, and hesitated as he saw a fireman standing beside him. He couldn't be sure this man was a slave of Tang-akhmut! He staggered to his feet and too late saw the swift sweep of the man's right hand, the blackjack that dangled in his palm. Wentworth's left arm went numb as he threw it up to ward the blow, the gun dropped from that hand. With his other weapons he fired from the hip. The bullet caught the man on the breastbone, drove him backward, feet groping woodenly for footing. For a moment he wavered on the unguarded edge of the balcony, then he pitched backward into space!

Wentworth whirled, left arm dangling, and leaped for the doorway of the dance hall. There could be no hesitation now, no delay in striking at the rubber-coated men. He had been a fool to think that the fire department could reach the scene so quickly! These were the men of Tang-akhmut, kidnapping those he had selected as his victims! Wentworth flung himself prone, the gun crashing out deadly lead. His first shot caught a man moving toward a window with a girl's limp body in his arms.

Before he could fire a second time, three of the false firemen whipped out revolvers and Wentworth was caught in a vicious cross fire. He laughed harshly. This was a language the Spider spoke better than they! He sped three bullets with the deliberation of target practice and three men were kicking out their lives on the floor!

In the street a whistle shrilled three times and the remaining men sprang to the windows, each snatching up a girl as he went. Not until then did Wentworth realize a half-dozen of the unconscious girls had been laid in a row against the wall, that these obviously had been selected for kidnapping along with many who had been carried out. Wrath rose brassily in his throat. He hurled to his feet, drew a bead on the fireman nearest a window and squeezed the trigger. The gun was empty!

Wentworth whirled to the unconscious police, searching for another weapon. There was none in sight. No time to hunt. Desperately he charged bare-headed on the escaping kidnappers! It was a mad, useless thing he did and a brave thing, but it was doomed to failure. No one man, even when that man was the Spider, could hope to battle victoriously the entire force of Tang-akhmut.

Pausing on a window-sill, one of the firemen leveled a gun point-blank and hammered out a drum roll of lead. Wentworth hit the floor before the first slug could reach him, counted the shots and was up and running at the last. Something broke against his chest with the miniature pop of a light bulb. He took another stride and his legs turned to rubber. He went down heavily and realized with his last conscious thought that the thing which had struck him had been a gas bomb. Even falling, he fought on. He hurled the empty gun into the face of the man who had thrown the bomb, saw him reel backward and catch the window-sill with the back of his knees, saw his legs point skyward, vanish. Then darkness swarmed thickly over the Spider's head.

CHAPTER 9
WHEN DWARFS MADE MERRY

WENTWORTH STRUGGLED up from the depths of unconsciousness with a feeling of overpowering danger, of intense urgency. He must come back now, *now!* He opened his eyes and gazed into blackness almost as intense as that into which the gas had plunged him. He was aware presently that he was still in the ballroom of the Sinton and that the light high above him on the ceiling came from the street. He pushed up dizzily from the floor. The senseless gas victims were about him in droves. He could not have been unconscious very long.

The struggle to achieve and maintain a balance on his feet was herculean. Across the littered room he reeled. The balcony still bore its burden of unconscious police but many streams of chemicals were pouring upon the smoldering embers of what had been the fire. Searchlights on fire trucks threw dazzling beams through open doors and windows. Across the lobby, Wentworth could catch the moving white gleam of interns' clothing as they hastened to reach the victims of Tang-akhmut's raid.

Little Wentworth could do here, little enough he could do anywhere. Tang-akhmut's Kentucky hideout was destroyed by this time. All that the Spider could do was wait until the instructions from Tang-akhmut reached the fathers of the kidnapped girls. Some of them, he recalled, would be summoned to witness a demonstration of the fate that awaited their daughters if they failed to comply with Tang-akhmut's demands!

When the fathers went to the rendezvous of the dwarfs, the Spider would go, too!

Already newspapers bore black banners which told of the night's horror. Twelve of the city's wealthiest heiresses had been carried off!

Wentworth had armed himself and taken ammunition from the unconscious police, but he hesitated now to approach alone the task that lay ahead—to overcome Tang-akhmut and his hordes single-handed; to free his victims. His strength was exhausted. Food and sleep he must have. It was not fear that prompted the Spider. But if he should fail, who would carry on in his stead? There was no answer. Heavily, Wentworth moved about further preparations for the battle. A drug store radio told him presently that the fathers of the kidnapped girls were meeting at the home of City Manager Reynolds, whose daughter was one of the victims. Wentworth had time to eat but not to sleep before he took up a watch there. From the tree outside from which he gazed into the window, Wentworth heard a phone bell ring, saw the men become excited. It was at once apparent that it was the city manager who had been summoned, for the others grouped about him and presently Reynolds moved heavily to the hall, returned with his hat in his hand.

Wentworth slid swiftly to the ground, raced through the shadows to the garage and hesitated beside two cars there, one a roadster, the other an expensive limousine designed to be chauffeur-driven. If he were right about the summons that had come for Reynolds being from Tang-akhmut, Reynolds would prefer to use the roadster. Wentworth hid in the rumble seat, closed it after him. A few moments later, the approach of heavy footsteps, the sag of the car on its springs, confirmed Wentworth's guess.

AT THE entrance to the roadway the car stopped, and Wentworth could hear City Manager Reynolds' grave voice. "If you have orders to follow me, men," he said, "I countermand them here and now. We must get our children back first of all."

Wentworth started at the nearness of the answering voice, just beside where he lay. "That's all right, sir. Our orders read like that, too."

The drive was a long one but finally it ended after a mile of rough road from which the dust sifted chokingly into the narrow cell Wentworth occupied. City Manager Reynolds' voice rang out sharply.

"Take me to Tang-akhmut at once!"

And all about the car, Wentworth heard the shrill giggling of the dwarfs! He heard Reynolds alight from the car and move off through a scuffling of dead leaves. Afterwards, there was silence. Slowly, Wentworth eased up the cover of the luggage compartment, spying through the crack. He could see nothing.

Still Wentworth moved cautiously, easing the cover back gradually. He climbed out and closed the rumble seat again, stole through the woods toward a shimmer of light that shone on the foliage of trees.

A high row of torches fastened to trees supplied the light and against the far side of the circular arena a throne chair had been placed. City Manager Reynolds stood beside it and on each side of him was a dwarf swinging one of the poison whips.

Except for that motionless group about the throne chair, the clearing was empty. On the chair was the sardonic figure of Tang-akhmut!

Wentworth drew a gun and checked the cylinder. It was full. He lay prone on the ground, the revolver ready. Reynolds stood between him and Tang-akhmut, but the moment the way was clear—Wentworth's lips hardened.

Tang-akhmut's voice reached him clearly. "Before we do anything at all, Reynolds," he said, "let me warn you that if for any reason I should so much as be hurt before this night is over, your daughter and her companions will share the fate I shall presently demonstrate for you. Just as they will if my demands for tribute are not met!"

Wentworth's face twitched. Slowly he eased down the hammer of his revolver. By those few words, Tang-akhmut had effectually put an end to all his plans.

Reynolds was facing Tang-akhmut. "I have no proof that my daughter is in your power," he said determinedly, "or that any of these other girls are. For all I know, you may be an impostor."

Tang-akhmut laughed. "I had anticipated some such attitude," he said. He touched the arm of his throne and in the woods a gong sounded. A dwarf ran out from the darkness, his arms heaped high with feminine apparel. It was all there, dresses and underclothing. Even stockings and slippers. These were thrown down at the feet of Reynolds, who stared at the pile with agonized eyes.

"Do you wish to examine the clothing?" Tang-akhmut asked with a mocking gentleness in his voice.

REYNOLDS WHIRLED about, his fists clenched. "Damn you, who has done this to those girls, stripped them of clothing...."

Tang-akhmut laughed and leaned forward. "I assisted with some! But most of it was done by my estimable assistants, the dwarfs!"

Reynolds' shoulders sagged. He turned away from the throne and looked down at the tumbled clothing. Wentworth forced himself to calm. His least movement might betray him—and he dared not harm Tang-akhmut!

"Now then," said Tang-akhmut clearly, "I am about to give you a little demonstration, my dear Reynolds. First of all, we will depict what already has happened to your so lovely daughter!"

A LEATHER whip cut into the flesh of Reynolds' face and left a bloody streak across his cheeks, across his mouth. Reyn-

THE SPIDER

olds flinched away. There was a thin smile on Tang-akhmut's lips. And from the darkness, a girl screamed.

There was a threshing and clatter in the underbrush that drowned even the thin laughter of the dwarfs and, a hunted thing, Clare Hubbell burst into the arena. *Clare!* Then she had been recaptured!

"In God's name!" she cried. "In God's name, Tang-akhmut, don't do this to me. I...."

Tang-akhmut lifted a hand, and from all sides of the arena a hideous pack of dwarfs rushed forward. They ran as eagerly as dogs, lips slack and drooling. They seized Clare and she started from their hands and tried to run. She struck at them. But they were all about her; their hands fastened on her clothing and the soft materials tore. Whips whistled and sang, bit into her shoulders.

"This," Tang-akhmut's voice rang, "is what already has happened. Now you shall see what fate awaits your daughter, Reynolds, *if you fail to obey!*"

Deliberately, Wentworth eased to his feet. The dwarfs had all congregated there to torture Clare, or a good part of them had. If, under cover of that uproar, he could circle the clearing and take Tang-akhmut prisoner....

Grimly, Wentworth clenched his revolver, his teeth set against heeding the cries of Clare Hubbell. It was one woman's fate against the lives of twelve, against the life of an entire city if Tang-akhmut continued at liberty. He had not weakened when Nita was menaced. He moved more swiftly, broke into a half-run in the darkness. Another dozen strides....

92

The crash of the revolver on the opposite side of the clearing scarcely rose above the clatter of the dwarfs, but to Wentworth it was the crack of doom—now, when he was so close to Tang-akhmut; when he was so close to victory again. As he raced on, frantic, Wentworth threw a single glance across the clearing. Just in the edge of the shadows stood a man with a revolver. He was pumping furious lead into the bodies of the dwarfs around Clare.

Clear above the turmoil, the man's voice rang out, "Clare! Clare! Come to me… This way. *This way!*"

The man was Adam Peck!

CHAPTER 10
ULTIMATUM OF DEATH

EVEN IN that instant of fierce action, Adam Peck's presence here was no mystery to Wentworth. It was plain that he had followed the same course Wentworth himself had pursued. Either in line of duty, or because he had some hint of the fate that awaited Clare, he had trailed Reynolds….

While that thought flashed across Wentworth's mind he was taking the one possible action which might snatch victory for them from the fiasco Adam Peck's untimely attack had threatened. If only Peck had delayed a few seconds longer, until Wentworth was just behind the throne….

Still, he dared not fire on Tang-akhmut—too many lives depended on his survival. Capture alone would suffice. Wentworth leaped into the open and spurted across the clearing toward the throne. As he ran, he fired twice. His bullets sped unerringly and the two dwarfs whose poison whips held Reynolds a helpless prisoner were blown into instant death.

"Reynolds!" Wentworth shouted. "Grab Tang-akhmut! Grab him. It's the only way to save your daughter!"

Reynolds stared, wildly confused for a moment. He twisted about and sprang for the throne—seconds too late. Tang-akhmut was not stupefied by horror. His mind grasped the danger instantly. His throne chair spun on a pivot. Wentworth's third hasty bullet, flung in despair at the Egyptian himself, clanged futilely on a metal shield which formed the back of the throne. Desperately, Wentworth strained the last ounce of speed from his legs. When he reached the spot a second later, the throne was empty! Nor was there any sound of retreat through the woods!

Yet from somewhere near, Tang-akhmut's voice called harshly. "It's the Spider! Kill the Spider!"

With a heave, Wentworth overturned dais and throne, but his half-formed suspicion that there was a hiding place beneath it proved groundless. He flung a glance toward the bedlam in the clearing and fired twice into the huddle of dwarfs, killed two who were hiding behind Clare's half-nude body. Peck's swiftly reloaded gun was taking care of the rest. The ground already was littered with the scattered corpses of Tang-akhmut's servitors. So much Wentworth saw in a single glance, then he hurled himself toward the underbrush where Tang-akhmut must be concealed.

For seeming hours, Wentworth scoured the woods in vain. If only Adam Peck had delayed his attack a few seconds longer!

No man could blame him for striking at the torturers of the girl he loved, but… Victory had been so near! When he returned to the clearing, all was silent except for the sobs of Clare Hubbell. Reynolds was slumped upon the overturned dais and in his hands was a torn, fragile dress. He looked at it dully, turning it over and over in his hands. Close in Peck's arms, his coat about her shoulders, Clare was slowly quieting. When he saw Wentworth, Peck left her and came forward slowly.

"I don't understand what I saw here a while ago," he said heavily, "but it proves I was wrong. I saw you kill four dwarfs. I saw you attack and try to kill Tang-akhmut, yet I swear I heard you make a deal with him as I told Captain Lacost. And I heard Tang-akhmut just a moment ago call you the Spider!"

Wentworth shook his head heavily. "You were hypnotized by Tang-akhmut," he said. "That is all. I think it would make my work a little easier, though, if you would gainsay your story to Lacost and get it in the newspapers and on the radio. We almost captured Tang-akhmut here…."

Peck's face went white. "Good God, you were circling to take him from behind, and I… if I had waited. God have mercy on me. I started a fight and because I did, those girls…."

"Don't say it!" Reynolds cried. "Tang-akhmut won't take vengeance on those poor helpless girls!"

WENTWORTH LOOKED down at the corpse-strewn ground. He shook his head. "Not in the way he intended, at least. If he has more dwarfs than these…" In all, the counted twenty of the twisted bodies on the ground. "We can do no more good here. Tang-akhmut has vanished long ago. Mr. Reynolds, Peck,

The identical thing happened to all
the bridges at the same moment.

go back to the city and take Clare with you. I'll remain and search a little longer."

Peck came forward sturdily. "I caused this mess and I'll help clean it up." He came close to Wentworth, pleading. "For God's sake, man, don't condemn me. Suppose that had been someone you love…."

"I'm not condemning you, Peck," Wentworth told him quietly. "But we must try to undo what has been done. Mr. Reynolds, will you take Clare back to the city, please?"

Reynolds was past voluntary thought. He nodded vacantly and stumbled toward his car. When he had gone, Wentworth and Peck returned to the clearing. Some of the torches had guttered out and there was little light left in the others. By what remained, Wentworth made a slow and thorough search of the bodies of the slain. If he hoped to find any evidence of the present hideout of Tang-akhmut, he was disappointed. There were marbles and bits of colored glass, bits of filched jewelry, such things as children might carry in their pockets. That was all. He rose stiffly to his feet after a while and crossed once more to the throne.

With Peck beside him, a powerful flashlight in his hand, he searched once more through the underbrush and this time Wentworth found what he sought. The side of a hollow tree had been swung on hinges. The interior was empty. It was plain that Tang-akhmut had hidden there until the search had passed, and then stolen away. Wentworth's woodcraft showed him the trail and eagerly the two men followed it—only to come to a blank wall at a concrete highway where Tang-akhmut plainly had entered an automobile.

"We can do no more now," Wentworth said quietly. "I know this road. It is a connecting link between two main highways. Both of them lead to Cincinnati and their other ends are the entire southern half of the United States...."

In the gray dawn, they entered Peck's car in which he had trailed Reynolds. Peck had gambled that Tang-akhmut was in Kentucky where he had been a prisoner, had watched the bridges and picked up the trail when Tang-akhmut's earlier vigilance against pursuit of Reynolds had been relaxed. Wentworth compelled a halt once, apparently to eat, actually to afford him a chance to renew his disguise.

Newspaper boys were already on the street, howling extras. Bold black letters across the pages told Wentworth the results of their abortive attack upon Tang-akhmut.

"Tang-akhmut Demands Whole City!"

"City Ransom Demanded for Girls!"

The headlines sounded ridiculously exaggerated, but when Wentworth read the context of the stories, he found the headlines were mild compared to the dictates of the enraged Tang-akhmut. Unless the Egyptian was at once named City Manager and Police Commissioner, guaranteed amnesty, and paid five millions of dollars, he would not only torture the twelve captive girls to death, but he would destroy the city! How this would be accomplished he did not state, but remembering the shattered water mains and their tragedy....

"Lest you doubt my ability to do this," said the statement

Tang-akhmut had given the commissioners of the city, "at five o'clock in the morning, on the dot, I shall destroy all bridges which connect this city with Kentucky!"

Wentworth, with a startled exclamation, stared up at the bridge that arched ahead of them toward Cincinnati. That, then, was the reason for the solid line of police which blocked the end of the span! They were determined to thwart Tang-akhmut in his plan. There were patrols along the river surface, airplanes overhead. Wentworth shook his head. They were doing all that could be done, but Wentworth knew it would not suffice.

AS THE thought crossed his mind, a big bell vibrated out the five strokes of the hour, and as each single note swept down the wind, the tension of the guards mounted. The airplanes hovered lower, speed boats on the river closed in on the piers. The last stroke sounded and, for a breath, over all that section of the earth rolled a great silence. It was broken by the roar of a racing automobile.

Before any one of the bridge guard could move, Wentworth sprang to the wheel of the auto that had brought them to the city, kicked the engine into life, turned the car around. He waited then, foot on the clutch pedal, while the machine whose engine had the deep note of power drew nearer. What Tang-akhmut's plan was, Wentworth did not know, but he was ready....

The car, whose engine Wentworth had heard, whirled in sight around a corner and he saw with a sense of utter unbelief that there was no one behind the wheel! The discovery stopped him only for a moment, then he started his own machine forward, headed it directly for the onrushing speedster, and leaped to the pavement. His old car rolled straight on, fairly in the path of the driverless machine! The crash seemed inevitable and Wentworth shouted a warning, hurled himself prone on the pavement. Explosion! That was it. The car was jammed with explosives!... An incredible thing happened! The powerful driverless car braked just enough to escape the collision, then charged on for the police line which blocked the bridge!

Instantly, guns opened fire on it, hammered on its sides, smashed the windshield—and did nothing more. For there was no driver to be shot! It had been no trick of the vision, then. *There was no one at the wheel of that car!*

It came to Wentworth belatedly that the car undoubtedly was controlled by radio. He shouted to the police, but to them it seemed supernatural. They sprang from its path and the mechanical monster dashed out onto the bridge. On and on it roared until it reached the highest point of the long span. At precisely the same instant, that identical scene was being enacted at the other two bridges across the Ohio River and, at precisely the same instant also, the driverless cars reached the middle... The detonation was overwhelming. In Cincinnati, the concussion tumbled an ancient apartment house in upon its foundations and Wentworth saw the tumbling brick, it seemed, before he saw the bottom fly out of the bridge, saw the girders tossed like jackstraws into the air, to go somersaulting slowly down into the river.

A hovering airplane, staggered, spurted straight up into the sky, then fluttered helplessly down and buried itself in the brown flood of the Ohio. A speedboat, guarding the main pier of the bridge, was buried under tons of masonry. Of that line of police that had guarded the entrance of the bridge, there was not one to be seen. The breath of the blast had hurled them into eternity. These were the first effects, the first minor movements of the explosions that rocked the cities on both sides of the river and shattered the windows as far back as Walnut Hill. The spans of the bridges, their middles torn out as neatly as if acetylene torches had burned them through, held up their stiff and useless arms like shocked monsters. But that was only for moments.

A cable supporting the suspension bridge snapped with a note of ten thousand bass viols and the whip-lash of it struck a building on the Kentucky shore and tore the side out of it, spilled it down into the street. Then the cracking, rending shriek of steel filled the air and the bridges bowed to their master, hid the ragged stumps of their arms in the river, subsided wholly into the flood, concealing their ineffective shattered steel beneath its brown depths.

When the last rumbling echo of the destruction died out, there was nothing of the bridges to be seen except the twisted scraps that thrust like black skeleton above the water, that and the shattered piers, the frothy gush of busted water mains. Wentworth, hurled a score of feet by the breath of that blast, had landed in the soft dirt of a vacant lot. He arose, staggering, and it was minutes before he could comprehend what had occurred. He searched for Peck, found him unconscious against a wall, but already beginning to stir. Together, they gazed at the wreckage and Wentworth felt the fury of his anger rise hot and burning within him. By God, there would be a vengeance!

THE DEVIL'S DEATH DWARFS

HIS CLENCHED fists sagged. He gripped his head. A vengeance, yes, but was he strong enough to inflict it? Petty victories he had had, yes, but had he, on any single point, proved himself the superior of this mighty Egyptian? The shock of the blast was hitting him harder now than it had in that first moment. Nausea punched his belly. He retched, sagged to the earth. It was a half hour before he could gather his strength to move, another hour before they could get a boat to carry them to the shores of the Ohio....

The shouting newsboys met them at the docks. The dead in the explosions so far had been counted at three hundred and fifty. The alternative to Tang-akhmut's ultimatum had been received. Let the city pay the five million dollars damages he demanded, let it surrender to him alive this animal who called himself the Spider, and Tang-akhmut would be merciful. He would return the girls unharmed, forget his demand that he head the city and the police. *He would not destroy the city!* But Richard Wentworth must be alive, alive and hearty. Tang-akhmut had not explained that request, but the newspaper interpreted it. Tang-akhmut meant to torture Wentworth with the slow cruelty of the East, torture him to death!

Wentworth stared at the sheet and the words blurred before his eyes. From that indistinct muddle, he seemed to see the dear face of Nita! Foolish to think that he could see her smile, mad to believe he could hear her voice! For Tang-akhmut intended her death with his. Of that there could be no doubt. He was striking back at Wentworth for his many oppositions, for the destruction of his dwarfs, for that other graver defeat in Kentucky.

103

Wentworth's lips twisted in a smile. Once more he could read the words. It seemed that Tang-akhmut was willing to make a concession. He was willing to surrender his own sister as a hostage, to be executed should he fail to keep his bargain! He would surrender her in exchange for Wentworth and the money—The girls would come later. He would hold them for twenty-four hours more to guarantee the city's good faith for that period of time.

Wentworth turned to Peck and there was an actual greatness in the smile of the Spider. "You had better leave me now," he told Peck softly.

Peck stood close to him. "Don't do it," he said harshly. "It is all trickery somewhere. Don't you realize that Nita."

Wentworth touched his arm. "Yes," he said, "and Tang-akhmut cares nothing for his sister. But you see, he gives the city only until noon! If he does not receive a pledge of submission by that time, he will *destroy the whole city!*"

"He can't," Peck cried stubbornly. "He couldn't do it! He..." He stopped then, for Wentworth was gazing at the stubs of the destroyed bridges. Peck's voice broke off with something close to a sob. "Damn it. Spider, you *can't!* Damn it, man, I..." He bowed his face into his hands and spoke through their muffling. "If you go into Tang-akhmut's hands I'll go, too. Maybe we can fight our way clear. Why, man..." He looked up. The Spider was gone!

Wentworth had merely run swiftly and silently to a nearby corner and strode along that street until he could make another turn. Peck might try to head him off, but he doubted it. Peck, too, should realize that there was nothing else to do. It was seven o'clock. There were five hours left. In five hours… Perhaps, if he could get in touch with Clare Hubbell and talk with her—He telephoned Reynolds' home, and Reynolds' answering voice was hoarse.

"Tang-akhmut took her away from me last night," he said savagely. "He stopped my car, he and his men… Afterward, he turned me free to bring his warning to the city. He just looked at me, and I couldn't do a thing. I never saw such eyes.…"

Wentworth hung up quietly. That hope was so soon finished! HE WENT out into the streets of the city. Somewhere here must lurk henchmen of Tang-akhmut, who, if he could find them, might be forced to reveal whatever secrets of the Egyptian they possessed. But almost certainly, they would know too little to lead Wentworth to victory as quickly as was necessary if he were to avert the destruction of the city. At the corner across the street a sign with large red letters had been placed on the sidewalk.

"No water in this area between Central and Wickerman, Fourth and Tenth. Water stations at.…"

A list of them was given, and out of the streets people walked heavy-footed, carrying buckets and bottles, kitchen pans to be filled. Two boys with a washtub on a toy wagon trudged slowly along the street and the lingering heat of summer beat down upon them. Over the whole area, there was a miasma of uncleanness. Streets had not been flushed and the very people on the streets seemed dusty and unwashed. The city had attempted to cleanse the sewers of the district, but where water was so scarce and the need merely for drinking purposes so great, the city work

105

THE SPIDER

accomplished little. Men worked in night-long shifts to build around the terrific breaks in the water mains, but Tang-akhmut had not been content to fracture any main a single time. His blasts had ripped them again and again, destroyed water gates so that whole additional areas must be cut off from important gates that controlled other mains than those smashed.

Already there had been a few isolated cases of typhoid. Hospitals were rushing supplies of typhoid serum, hoping to check epidemics; there had been three well-defined cases of cholera and all of the victims had died. And Wentworth knew the tale of horror was only beginning! Suppose Tang-akhmut struck without further warning; suppose he smashed the water mains of the entire city, wrecked its water supply!

Some emergency relief could be contrived at once, of course; trains bringing in tank cars of water. But it would be a week, perhaps a month before full facilities could be restored. And in the meantime, men and women would go thirsty and dirty; disease would spread. And there was the ever-present threat of fire. Let the smallest blaze start anywhere in the waterless areas and it would be almost impossible to stop it. Chemicals would work if the thing was discovered in time. Indeed, the city had motorcycle patrols of chemical equipment going the rounds ceaselessly. But let a fire get beyond their weak control, and it might sweep for blocks before dynamite could check it!

If Tang-akhmut were intent on quick destruction of the city, he need only destroy the mains and start a half-dozen small fires. Morning would find the city smoking amid its ruins!

Irresistibly drawn, Wentworth strode along the barren streets where stench and heat simmered up to the sky. One man had done all this, caused the suffering and the disease. And he had done it only for the end that he might enrich himself. Fresh hatred of Tang-akhmut spurred Wentworth....

Distantly a bell tolled. Time had passed since he entered the city. Eleven o'clock. And by noon, Tang-akhmut must receive assurance that Wentworth would be surrendered.

Across the street from him, an old woman moved with the weight of her years along the street. In her right hand she clutched a tiny saucepan almost full of water. As she walked, she glanced furtively about her as if this burden she bore were so precious that other eyes than hers must not gaze upon it. A dog with lolling tongue slunk along the building front, darted at a pool of filthy water in the gutter and lapped eagerly. The woman clasped her water to her and stole away.

THE ATTACK was furious and without warning. A man leaped from a doorway, struck once and was gone with the little pan of water into the darkness from which he had come. On the pavement, the old woman did not move. Wentworth ran to her side, gun in hand.

Unless, all so useless. The man was a beast, but it was another and viler beast who had caused this—Tang-akhmut! Wentworth bent over the old woman. She was still alive. He picked up her emaciated body and strode back the way he had come until he reached the edge of the waterless area. A long queue of people with vessels for water waited beside a fire plug where men guarded by policemen doled out the fluid. And the people cried out as Wentworth walked to the plug with the woman in his arms, cried out not in pity or in horror, but at the fact that some one was going ahead of their waiting line to receive life-giving water!

Wentworth did what he could for the old woman, had her carried to a hospital, and found that his time was short. If he were to surrender... That was madness. What other course was open to him? A city facing such desolation as he had glimpsed this morning? Suppose even that scanty relief, the long queues at the fire plug were gone? He moved swiftly across the city, entered the police headquarters and made his way unmolested to the office of the city detectives, the big room where they wrote their reports and lounged when there was nothing to do. Wentworth stood staring at the floor, a lithely powerful man whose head still sat his shoulders with arrogance, whose lips could twist whimsically or grow bitter thin. He went quietly to the door that opened on the private office of Captain Lacost and knocked lightly.

"Come in!" the man shouted.

Wentworth stepped in and stood quietly just inside. There was irascibility in Captain Lacost's glare, which was directed at three of the city commissioners.

"There's no use talking any more! You can remove me or do any other damned thing you want!" He was on his feet, pounding the desk. "I tell you that even if we find the Spider, we won't turn him over to that damned fiend, Tang-akhmut. We won't! It's contrary to the law in the first place, and in the second place... Damn it, I *like* the guy. What little there was done to protect those girls at the Sinton, he did. He was responsible for our being there, he warned us about the gas masks, told us when the gas had been released. It wasn't his fault that he didn't know the gas would penetrate a mask. Now, damn you, until you kick me out, this is my private office and I don't want you in it. Get out!" He whipped toward Wentworth. "What the hell do you want?"

Wentworth smiled at him slowly and began to remove with swift hands the details of his facial disguise! His shoulders straightened and the devil-may-care carriage of his head was there again, the reckless glint of his eyes. When he had finished, he faced the silent men.

"I am Richard Wentworth, wanted for murder and on charges of being the Spider," he said quietly. "I have come to surrender myself to you so that you can ransom the city from Tang-akhmut... with my body!"

CHAPTER 11
IN TANG-AKHMUT'S LAIR

CAPTAIN LACOST jumped from behind his desk. "You damned fool!" he cried at Wentworth. "You poor damned fool!" His voice went suddenly husky. He whirled on the city commissioners. "You want to surrender a man like this to Tang-akhmut! Damn you, I'd rather turn you all over than this one! He's all *man!*"

The city commissioners were gray of face. "It isn't," their spokesman said, "especially a matter of what we want. It's what Tang-akhmut says we must do. The destruction of the bridges this morning proves what he can do."

"Precisely," Wentworth said. "May I suggest that you notify Tang-akhmut at once that I have surrendered and that you will be ready to meet his terms at midnight? Insist on that delay. I wish you would tell him that I surrendered. It's my vanity, I suppose, but I wouldn't want the beggar to think I'm afraid of him."

The commissioners grasped Wentworth's hand one by one, filed from the office. Captain Lacost glowered at him, turned his back and strode to the window. He blew his nose. "What in the hell do you expect to gain by a twelve-hour delay?"

"It will give you time to summon national guardsmen," Wentworth said quietly. "Regular army men, the marines, would be even better. Fortify the city. If there is any slip-up at all, Tang-akhmut will wipe out the city just as he threatens. I'm not convinced that he won't do that anyway after I have surrendered. Destroy and loot the city by destroying the water mains and starting a few fires."

"I've already demanded the national guard," Lacost said shortly. "Perhaps regular army men would be better. I'll order a search of the water mains for bombs and so on, if you think it will help. I personally think that bombs are introduced into the mains at some point and timed to explode later. Any other suggestions?"

Wentworth urged a redoubled fire patrol, a guard of planes to shoot down any craft that failed to heed their order not to fly over the city.

"And I want Hal Shields of the *Times-Post* sent here," Wentworth finished.

"Shields, eh?" Lacost rumbled. "He's the guy that accused you, him and Peck. I damned near busted Peck for that, but he seemed so sure of what he'd heard—"

"Hypnosis," Wentworth explained briefly. "He doesn't believe it now. I'd like to talk with Shields over the phone first."

It was arranged, and Wentworth demanded to know what Shields had accomplished in the line of investigation that had been outlined to him long ago, a survey of possible suspects in whose identity Tang-akhmut might be masquerading. Wentworth had no clue to go on. Tang-akhmut was carefully preserving such identity, granted that he had one, for purposes of escape. How simple, with an identity established, simply to cease being Tang-akhmut and assume that identity until such time as he chose to initiate his horrors again in some other locality.

Wentworth thought grimly that there was no need of Tang-akhmut hiding. If Wentworth failed in the plan that was beginning to take form in his brain, Tang-akhmut would be undisputed ruler of the city. He might destroy it and move his sinister hordes to another scene of activity; or he might milk the city dry of wealth. There might be opponents, but Wentworth doubted that any one of them could stand against the genius of the Egyptian. When the Spider failed....

SHIELDS CAME shame-facedly to police headquarters. "I want to apologize for the things we printed about you, Mr. Wentworth," he said firmly. "Any man who could do the brave thing you have done...."

Wentworth brushed it aside. "Time is short," he said. "Tell me everything you have learned." He relaxed in his chair and

With the fury of exploding dynamite Wentworth flung himself headlong on Tang-akhmut.

113

closed his eyes. Weariness was upon him, the fatigue of sleepless nights, of long travail. But he drove his brain to the task ahead without remitting, without pause.

Shields' voice ran on clearly. "Fielding, the commissioner of public works, in charge of water mains, is a logical suspect. He was in financial straits recently, but seems to have recouped himself. The kidnapping or death of Willa Abel might have been a blind to make it seem that some one outside the department was responsible."

Wentworth moved impatiently. Except for Clare Hubbell's admission that Willa was still alive, he had been unable to find any trace of the girl. Yet Clare's treachery in betraying him to Tang-akhmut seemed to point to some hold over her.

"I'm not interested in proof that any individual man might be responsible for the crimes of Tang-akhmut," he said shortly. "Tang-akhmut is guilty... The man I am seeking would be a man to whom no blame could attach, whose identity Tang-akhmut can assume at the proper time without any possibility of being suspected; an identity he can use as a safer hiding place than any secret lair."

Shields was silent for moments. "Then I have failed entirely," he said. "All that I have discovered points to certain men as guilty, or as possible allies of Tang-akhmut. That was what you wanted, as I understood—men who might be used as scapegoats by Tang-akhmut."

Wentworth opened his eyes, smiled. "You are right, Shields," he said. "Forgive my impatience. I did ask for that information.

It is only that my ideas of Tang-akhmut's plans have undergone a revision. Go on with your list."

Shields listed Fritz Maddern, who had disappeared from his usual places of operation.

"Probably dead," Wentworth interjected. "Killed by Tang-akhmut."

"Adam Peck," Shields said heavily, "in conjunction with Clare Hubbell."

Wentworth smiled his appreciation of Shields' utter fairness. Shields was wildly in love with Clare Hubbell, yet he could add her to the list.

"Myself and Clare Hubbell," Shields pushed on. "I helped Tang-akhmut's plans by the publishing of that story with Peck. That's all the list, Mr. Wentworth."

Wentworth jerked to his feet, strode back and forth across the office. "I want a picture of Willa Abel and a close description," he said swiftly. "It's important, and there isn't much time!"

Shields stared at him. "I don't understand…."

"I don't myself," Wentworth snapped at him. "Hurry!"

Shields was back inside an hour and Wentworth pored over the pictures and information he brought. He built up such a picture of Willa Abel that—so far as the descriptions went—would enable him to pick her out instantly his eyes fell upon her. Adam Peck entered before he was finished and Wentworth called on him for further details.

"But what is this all about?" Lacost demanded harshly. "It don't make sense to me."

Wentworth shook his head impatiently. "I'm only playing a

wild hunch," he said sharply. "One that has possibility in fact, but may be far from the truth. It is my only hope…" He relaxed abruptly, feeling the weariness sweep over him. It was seven o'clock, and at midnight….

"I want to sleep for three hours," he said quietly. "I want my brain rested for tonight."

A COT was set up in the office and Wentworth flung himself upon it, plunged instantly into deep sleep. It was dark when he awoke. In a chair beside his bed sat Adam Peck, eyes burning into the darkness before him. Wentworth stretched luxuriously.

"What time is it, Peck?" he asked quietly.

Peck started violently. "Two minutes after ten," he said finally.

Wentworth swung his feet to the floor. "I feel like eating. Any place near here…" He stopped, laughing. "I guess I'm a prisoner at that. How about sending out for food? A condemned man…."

Peck said violently, "Go to hell!" He hurled from the room and after a while came back more quietly. Dinner was served for the two of them and the captain came in and smoked a rank cigar. Wentworth insisted that no attempt was to be made to interfere with Tang-akhmut. He was given, at his request, two thin pieces of tempered steel, which he fastened to the palms of his hands, concealed under bits of flesh-colored court plaster.

Peck said furiously: "Wentworth, it isn't too late. I can tie up Captain Lacost and we'll climb out the window."

"I'm willing!" Lacost bit hard on his cigar. "But you'll have to find some other means of exit than the window!"

Wentworth walked slowly to the window. Beneath it, filling the street from wall to wall, was a dense crowd.

"Isn't it time to leave for our rendezvous?" he asked shortly.

Captain Lacost got to his feet. "Listen, Wentworth, what Peck says is right. We've got the guards all set, national guards and army. We've won the delay we needed. Let's go hunt down this fiend. I'm going with you!"

Wentworth shook his head. "I'm not surrendering as a blood sacrifice, captain," he said quietly. "Your guards may or may not prevent destruction of the city this time. But until Tang-akhmut is dead the danger will hover over the city. Sooner or later, he will succeed. And many lives will be lost. As I said, I'm not going into this blindly. I have a plan...."

Lacost scowled at him, but seemed half-convinced. Men were accustomed to expect miracles of the Spider! Wentworth smiled, lest his sober face reveal how slight was his plan and how slim his chance of success!

"Come on!" he said, almost gaily it seemed, "Let's go out and meet Tang-akhmut!"

OUTSIDE THE office, men were silent, too, and Wentworth walked between throngs that made no sound as he left the building and entered a waiting car. Only when the machine moved away, the voice of the mob rose in a sound that was sob and cheer together. Wentworth settled back in his seat. His plan depended on freedom within the headquarters of Tang-akhmut, on finding out certainly if Willa Abel lived or was dead. Of course, if he could destroy Tang-akhmut... He shook his head. He was buoying himself up with day-dreams. If only Nita were not a prisoner of Tang-akhmut!

He twisted about. "Captain, try to make him surrender Nita van Sloan to you! If only you can get her safely—"

The captain shifted the cold cigar to the opposite mouth corner. "We tried," he said flatly.

After perhaps a half hour's drive, the car pulled to the side of the road. For a while they had had an escort of other cars, but now they had dropped far back. Presently a limousine passed at high speed. A green light blazed from its rear window and instantly the car Wentworth occupied fell in behind it. For another half hour they traveled swiftly until the surrounding hills closed in and became wooded and lonely, then there was an abrupt turn to the right over a jouncing dirt road. The car ahead stopped and men got out. Wentworth's party alighted also and began hauling out packages of money from the luggage compartment.

Wentworth nodded pleasantly to the woman who came toward them, recognizing Tang-akhmut's sister, Issoris, who was to be hostage for Tang-akhmut's word. Her head was held proudly erect, but there was a paleness in her cheeks.

"Cheer up," Wentworth greeted her. "If you are killed, it will at least be quickly!"

She bit her lip, and the men with her began to throw the packages of money into their own car. In a few moments the task was done and they stood staring impassively at Wentworth. They were new faces to him, none of the freakish servitors he usually connected with Tang-akhmut, but ordinary gunmen killers. They gestured him into the back of the car, locked his feet to a foot rest, cuffed his hands together and sprang into the front seat. Instantly, the car got under way. The police machine did not follow.

After jouncing over the rough road for a few minutes, the car hit smooth pavement and turned northward. Wentworth composed himself to wait, rested against the trials ahead. So much depended on so little, his freedom within the headquarters of Tang-akhmut first of all. Perhaps Nita might know the answer he sought. If, having learned that, he could escape and defeat Tang-akhmut's plans, destroy his hordes and force Tang-akhmut to take cover. . . .

It took a full hour to reach the spot that Tang-akhmut had chosen for a rendezvous, an hour of endless twisting and doubling on the trail. At the end of that time, Wentworth's feet were unlocked and he was led up rough stone steps to a house atop a bluff. One man on each side gripped his arms and his hands had been cuffed in front of him.

Wentworth was thrust into a window-less room, manacled with ankle irons to a ring in the floor and roughly searched. Then the men went away. Within three minutes they were back, and they examined the palms of Wentworth's hands, ripped away the court plaster that concealed his miniature tools! Wentworth felt his mouth grow grim. He had been a fool to think the same trick would work twice on Tang-akhmut! It was a half hour later that Wentworth heard gunfire crash out nearby, heard the answering yammer of machine guns. A moment later, Tang-akhmut stalked into the room. He stood with his great yellow eyes glowing fiercely. He wore the striped robes of the Pharaoh and on his head was the Crown of the Two Niles.

"YOU THOUGHT you could trick me, did you?" he cried out harshly. "You thought your men could follow and trap us! Well, they are wrong. They shall be trapped! And because of this treachery, the city shall be destroyed!" Tang-akhmut laughed. Men freed Wentworth's feet and trained guns on him.

"Now, march, fool!" Tang-akhmut ordered.

Wentworth moved silently forward. His time was not yet. Meantime, patience and watchfulness. The way led into the cellar, through a trap door where a dozen men waited. There were electric buttons in the walls and when one was pressed, a machine gun yammered up above.

"All come with me except Slade," Tang-akhmut ordered. "Slade, when they are inside, press the two-minute button and follow us."

The man called Slade nodded with a crooked grin and the others surrounded Wentworth and hustled him down through a long and twisting passageway. He was heartsick for the attacking party, but helpless to assist them. After what seemed an interminable time there was a dull rumbling far above them and a little dirt sifted down from the ceiling of the tunnel.

"That was the end of the attacking party!" Tang-akhmut hissed his words. "United States marines, I believe. But even marines are vulnerable to nitro-glycerin in sufficient quantities!"

Wentworth felt his face grow rigid, but he held his peace. Useless to rage at Tang-akhmut. He had to gain a little time presently....

They arrived finally at a chamber hollowed out of living rock. Off at one end was a narrow opening to the grayness

120

of approaching dawn. Tang-akhmut touched some button and a roseate light slowly waxed until it filled the chamber. Wentworth's eyes flashed about and his heart leaped. Nita was here... Ah, but it could only mean torture, her presence. She was chained to the opposite wall among the drooping figures of a dozen other girls. Swiftly, Wentworth's eyes canvassed them. They were the debutantes who had been kidnapped and Willa Abel was not among them. Well, he had not really expected she would be....

Nita gazed proudly into Wentworth's eyes, a little smile about her lips. It said more plainly than words that she had known he would come; that he could not have done otherwise. Wentworth smiled back with stiff lips. Nita was so brave... and their chances were so slim!

Tang-akhmut was gloating. He could not keep the laughter from his lips. "I warned the fools in Cincinnati not to attempt treachery," he cried. "I promised that the city should be destroyed if I were opposed. And there was treachery, blackest treachery. That it failed does not matter. Did you expect it to succeed?" He strode up to confront the manacled Wentworth.

Wentworth slowly shook his head. "Certainly not," he said quietly.

"Are you trying to tell me that you advised against treachery?" Tang-akhmut demanded incredulously.

Wentworth smiled slightly. "I merely answered your question, Tang-akhmut!"

Tang-akhmut whirled away, strode across to his chained captives. Wentworth's lid-masked eyes saw that the rock chamber was carefully guarded. There were fully a dozen men stationed about its walls and at its exits, all of them with guns; four of them with machine guns. But it was a poor showing for Tang-akhmut, he who usually held grand court with Negro slaves and silken drapes about him. And Wentworth knew that he himself was responsible for this—and that Tang-akhmut knew it and would make him pay accordingly—him and Nita.

But had Tang-akhmut other men? Was he depending on these few to destroy the city? Properly used, of course, they could do it, but it was not like Tang-akhmut to risk everything thus on one throw of the dice. The essence of his strategy was to have double, triple safeguards on everything....

Tang-akhmut was jeering at the captives. "I promised your parents that you would die by slow fire," he said, "and I like to keep my promises. One of your number I shall permit to die here before we leave! The others... the others shall help to destroy the city for me! Flaming torches from the sky!"

WENTWORTH'S EYES stared narrowly about him, at Tang-akhmut. The man was mad, utterly mad, but his was the power. God help the world when a madman seized the power! And Wentworth recognized that madness such as Tang-akhmut's was not weakness but strength. Tang-akhmut had thrown his hands above his head, shouting words in a strange, guttural tongue which Wentworth recognized with a start as the language of the dwarfs! God, were there more of those little monsters alive!

From a shadowy corner of the room four of them ambled forward, two of them carrying pails. They clustered around

Tang-akhmut, waiting for orders, and the Egyptian pointed to one of the shrinking girls. Her screams rose maddeningly. Wentworth peered about and the faces of some of the guards were gray and wet with perspiration. Tang-akhmut might dominate these men by greed and fear, but they were no such servants to him as the dwarfs had been. These men would not hesitate to kill a woman or women who stood in their path, but torture… Wentworth shook his head. If he hoped to stir them to revolt against Tang-akhmut, his plan was foredoomed. They would fear the Egyptian too mightily!

The girl had been dragged from the rock-secured gyves and thrown to the ground. Over her feet, over her extended arms, one of the dwarfs was slopping liquid from a pail. The acrid stench of oil came to Wentworth's nostrils. Wentworth lifted his voice.

"Tang-akhmut!" he cried. "Tang-akhmut, why destroy your great name!"

The Egyptian whirled angrily about, saw that it was Wentworth who had spoken, and strode toward him.

"Shall it be said that the great Pharaoh, Tang-akhmut," Wentworth continued, "tortured women to death out of petty spite? That he failed to seize a city and so tortured a few helpless women in his hands?"

Tang-akhmut struck Wentworth heavily across the face with the palm of his hand. "Dog, do you dare to address me, unbidden!"

Wentworth stared into the blazing eyes of Tang-akhmut. "Only for my own sake and yours," he said curtly. "I would not have it said that I was beaten by a man who was only a torturer of women! You should have more pride...."

Tang-akhmut stood smiling thinly upon him. "So you suppose that I shall not destroy the city, too? Wentworth, you underestimate me! I tell you the mines are already set beneath the water mains. In half a hundred places over the city, my fires are laid. There are control keys here. I need only press one of them to destroy the entire city of Cincinnati by fire and thirst and disease!"

He must have glimpsed the hope that sprang into Wentworth's eyes, the hope he gained from the knowledge that the control key was within this room. Tang-akhmut laughed. "Ah, no, Wentworth. Even if you could escape from your bonds, even if you could overcome all my men and slay me, you could not save the city. Besides the key here, there are three others hidden in various retreats of mine. And there is a time device which at high noon today will work my will even if I and all my men are destroyed!"

The words struck like swords to Wentworth's heart. Here indeed was the death of all his hopes! Even if he could destroy Tang-akhmut, the city would perish....

Tang-akhmut struck Wentworth again across the face. "Do you dare to call me still a mere torturer of women?" he jeered.

Perhaps it was desperation that seized Wentworth then. Perhaps the galvanic response of his brain to the one opportunity for life and rescue of the city. For all his vaunted strength and his precautions, Tang-akhmut had made two mistakes. He had stepped too close to Wentworth when his hands were

124

tied before him; he had allowed one of his dwarfs to play with fire. With the fury of a dynamite explosion Wentworth flung himself headlong upon Tang-akhmut and drove his doubled fists beneath the Egyptian's chin!

CHAPTER 12
BORN IN FLAMES

WENTWORTH'S ATTACK, bound as he was and in the face of tremendous odds, took Tang-akhmut and his armed guards so much by surprise that for a space of seconds after he struck, they froze, staring. If it had not been for the fact that the Egyptian, struck beneath the chin by Wentworth's two-fisted blow, had been hurled to the ground, they would have been more inclined to laugh than to shout with alarm. But the Spider, as always, had acted with keen foresight. The instant his fists thudded home, he was springing into the second maneuver of his desperate bid for freedom, for the salvation of a city!

A single stride brought him abreast of the dwarf who held the torch tauntingly over the oil-soaked body of the girl. Wentworth seized the torch with both hands, kicked the dwarf into insensibility. An instant later, he had hooked up a bucket of oil on his toe and hurled it directly at Tang-akhmut! In a sweeping semi-circle, the oil swept across the floor of the cavern. A single gunman fired at Wentworth then, the shot echoed and re-echoed thunderously across the cavern. Wentworth threw back his head and laughed, a deep mocking note. With both hands he lifted the blazing torch above his head. Men screamed then, understanding what he meant to do. Tang-akhmut made a desperate effort to regain his feet, his mouth open in a soundless shout as he faced death by the means he had ordained for his victims.

Directly at Tang-akhmut, Wentworth flung the torch!

Tang-akhmut found his voice now. It rang out, hoarsely terrified. He batted at the torch with a frantic hand, knocked it to the floor, and instantly flame ran like a scarlet serpent across the cavern. The blaze leaped high, slicing the chamber in half, separating the captors from the captives. Through the crackle and roar of the conflagration, Wentworth could hear the shrill screaming of Tang-akhmut!

For a moment Wentworth stood motionless, staring at the barrier his shrewdness had erected. But it would die soon, even as he hoped Tang-akhmut was dying now, and before that time, he must be free. He stooped to drag the girl from the path of flames, took the second bucket half full of oil and set it aside, ready when the first should begin to die. He cast a brief smiling glance at Nita and set to work on his wrist bonds with his teeth....

Even while he attacked the ropes, his mind was swiftly canvassing his situation. If he had read aright the men who fought beside Tang-akhmut, they were more than half terrified by the Egyptian's threats. If Tang-akhmut had fallen and the menace before them seemed at all dangerous, the Spider believed they would desert. As he gnawed, Wentworth's eyes quested about for weapons. One of the dwarfs, fleeing before the fire, had dropped a poison whip. Over beyond the fire there had been a few sporadic shots, now silence. Wentworth hurled the second bucket of oil into the trickle that fed the fire and hurried along the wall toward the dark shadow from which the dwarfs had advanced.

The heat in the cavern was becoming intense, but there was nothing save the oil on which the flames could feed. And the slope of the cavern floor was away from the gyved victims against the wall, as Wentworth had perceived before he had taken his desperate chance. But before the flames died out entirely, he must have adequate weapons and be in a position to free the prisoners…Wentworth's straining arms snapped the last strand of his bonds.

For once fortune seemed to favor the Spider. The shadow he penetrated proved to be a narrow passageway which led directly into a storage room. There were a score of torture contrivances concealed there and, more important, a store of arms. Wentworth snatched out a half dozen automatics which he thrust into pockets and belt, hurriedly broke out a box of ammunition. WHEN FINALLY the oil-fed flames died, Wentworth with Nita freed and crouched beside him, waited with ready automatics—and found no enemy before him. Whether the men of Tang-akhmut had thought the captives doomed by Wentworth's rash attack with fire, or whether Tang-akhmut's fall had robbed them of courage, they had fled while still the oil blazed. Feverishly then, Wentworth turned to the task of freeing the prisoners, of leading them from the cavern toward the daylight whose color had turned from gray to gold with the rising sun.

He entrusted them to Nita. "Hurry back to the city and tell

the police what you heard Tang-akhmut tell me—that the entire city faces destruction at noon! Tang-akhmut said there was a key here. If I can find it and trace wires to one of the mines beneath the water mains, it may be possible to prevent them from being blown up and the fire bombs from being exploded. It is a slim chance...."

Nita stood quietly to take Wentworth's commands, and when they were finished she laid a pleading hand on his arm.

"Dick, must we be separated again?" she whispered. "Death has been so close. And I feel here, here in my heart, that death is still close to you! Come with me, Dick...."

Nita's words taunted Wentworth's muscles. Sharply, he peered into the shadows of the cavern. Nita was not given to idle concern, nor would she warn him without reason.

"My duty lies here, yours in the city," he said quietly. "I will follow as swiftly as possible, dear. If I can't find the key here, if the police can't find the mines in the city, then the city must be evacuated! There is only a matter of three or four hours before the time-key which Tang-akhmut set will start the destruction of the city, even if he and all his men are dead!"

Reluctantly, Nita turned away with her charges and Wentworth raced into the search of the cavern. Heat penetrated the soles of his shoes and the air was suffocatingly thick with fumes. If he failed to find the contact key which Tang-akhmut had boasted would destroy the city—

Even as he searched, Wentworth was beginning to realize the futility of the thing he sought to do. If he found the key immediately and a crew was set to work tracing the wire to its other end in a mine of explosives, it was scarcely possible they could locate the first of the charges before the automatic detonator touched it off. Yet if they failed in that attempt….

The full picture of the horror Tang-akhmut planned sickened Wentworth. In one moment, Tang-akhmut would destroy all means of fighting fire and at the same time start more blazes than the fire department could hope to subdue. Good God, they would not be able to check a tenth of the fires! Whatever Tang-akhmut's faults, lack of thoroughness was not one of them. His fires would be started by incendiary bombs which would rip fire through buildings as swiftly as a gasoline explosion.

Wentworth's lips tightened thinly. He whirled and strode purposefully from the cavern. There was only one thing to do. The city must be evacuated before Tang-akhmut struck! The search for the mines, for the wires that would bring the fatal spark to the explosives and incendiaries must go on, but the only safety of the city's thousands lay in flight. Many men would have deemed the task hopeless even before begun, but it was not in Wentworth to give up, though the odds against success were incredible. In three to four hours, to warn and empty a city of four hundred thousand souls!

ONE THING Wentworth found in his favor when he returned to Cincinnati by means of a car he had commandeered at gunpoint on the road: the city was under martial law. He had already telephoned to Captain Lacost of the detectives and revealed the dilemma of the city. While he strove to make Lacost realize the peril, the necessity of immediate action, Nita van Sloan and her charges had arrived at police headquarters, all adding their confirmation of Tang-akhmut's threat. Lacost promised to go at once to City Manager Reynolds, whose daughter was restored to him, and to Brigadier General Haley, in charge of the troops that patrolled the city.

"But it is a hopeless task!" Lacost cried. "To empty a city of four hundred thousand in a few hours' time! It will take longer than that to arrange transportation!"

Wentworth felt the cold fury that he had known of old take hold of him—when men said things were impossible and sat back and flapped helpless hands… This day, Richard Wentworth knew that he faced his greatest task, his greatest travail. Under charges that would mean his death on arrest, he must nevertheless force his way into the presence of General Haley, of City Manager Reynolds and force them into violent action. And he must do this either in his own identity, or in that of the Spider. To either, these men might listen, certainly to no one else.

So it was, half an hour later, Richard Wentworth, without disguise, leaped from his car at military headquarters, established at the Gibson House hotel. Wentworth himself held a rank of major in the reserve; he knew procedure.

"Major Wentworth," he told the sergeant of the guard, "with orders to report directly to General Haley without delay!"

It was not strange that these soldiers did not recognize the calmly authoritative man before them. Major Wentworth did not mean to them a hunted felon, but an officer whose commands they would gladly accept. Possibly Captain Lacost, if he had heard the orderly's whispered word to General Haley, would have guessed, but he saw only Haley's frown of hesitation.

Wentworth had deliberately phrased his message ambiguously. General Haley might well think that he brought personal orders from the Governor....

Two minutes later, Wentworth was ushered into the presence of the captain of detectives and the commander of the martial forces in the city. Lacost jumped to his feet with a glad cry, sprang forward to offer his hand.

"Wentworth!" he shouted. "By God, I'm glad you're here. I can't convince General Haley...."

Wentworth pivoted toward the general, ignoring military formality. "General," he said crisply, "this city must be evacuated at once. It must be done without delay for organization, without appointing rendezvous or objectives. Believe me, if you hesitate for one hour, the deaths of thousands of persons will be laid at your door!"

General Haley's jaw jutted. "You obtained entrance here by a trick, Major Wentworth, if that is your name!"

Wentworth nodded quietly. "It is my name. I am Richard Wentworth." He mentioned regiment and service briefly. "Captain Lacost will tell you that the police are convinced that I am the Spider."

Haley thudded to his feet. *"Orderly!"* he shouted.

Wentworth did not draw a weapon. "General, if you order out the guard, I shall be compelled to shoot both you and the orderly!" He said the words quietly, but with a grim emphasis that could not be misunderstood. "Your life, the life of every officer in the brigade is infinitely less important than the salvation of the city!"

THROUGH A long minute the eyes of the two men held. The orderly entered and stood quietly waiting. In General Haley's eyes, Wentworth read first anger, then a slow and grudging admiration.

"You would be willing to go to those lengths?" he said quietly, at last. "You are convinced utterly then that these things you urge are necessary?"

"I tell you that unless this city is largely cleared by noon," Wentworth said, "fully half the population will die either by fire or panic. At noon, precisely, Tang-akhmut will blow up the water mains and detonate scores of incendiary bombs. Fire will sweep the city! There will be nothing to check it!"

General Haley slowly straightened, a grim smile twitching the long line of his mouth. "You have a forceful way of presenting your arguments, Major," he said quietly. "Orderly, call an immediate meeting of my full staff. I want every man here and waiting in five minutes."

When the orderly had gone, Haley remained on his feet. "I am curious to know, Major, whether you would have carried out your threat to shoot?"

Wentworth smiled slightly, his eyes on the frosty blue eyes of the general. After a moment, Haley nodded slowly and dropped into his seat. He dragged the palms of his hands across the blotter.

"What are your recommendations, Major?" he asked abruptly.

Whether it was the conviction that Wentworth was absolutely sincere in his determination, hence that he believed in the necessity of the thing he urged; or whether is was Wentworth's rigid insistence that Haley would be held responsible by the government if he failed to heed a plain warning that disaster threatened, General Haley was persuaded. With staccato phrases, he divided the city into swift sections, dispatched the troops in his command with orders to empty the houses in that area and move them as rapidly as possible beyond the outskirts of the city.

"At noon," he finished his orders harshly, "the city must be clear. At that time, this villain, Tang-akhmut, will destroy Cincinnati!"

Haley prepared to remain at the Gibson until the last possible moment to set up a telephonic liaison with the various detachments, to arrange for food and supplies to follow behind each company as it pushed the populace out of the city. It was a tremendous job of organization, efficiently and powerfully undertaken. Wentworth had worked out the details of the plan during his dash to headquarters. When asked for suggestions, he had them ready in detail and the General was forced to fresh admiration for his efficiency.

"I'm sorry to have to put you under arrest, Major Wentworth," he said finally. "The technical charge is threatening a superior officer in time of emergency. Actually, of course, I am holding you for the police."

Wentworth bowed. "If you will accept my parole, general," he said, "there is a great deal of work to be done that I believe I can do best."

General Haley shook his head sharply. "You know I can't do that, Wentworth!"

Wentworth smiled slightly. His hand moved fleetly and an automatic gleamed dully in his fist. "I have to warn you, gentlemen, not to move. What I have to do for the city, I will do. Nothing shall stop me!"

Captain Lacost laughed out loud. General Haley smiled a very little. "If you state your proposition that way," he said quietly, "we will have to remain quietly here until you have made good your escape. Good luck, Major Wentworth!"

A WARM smile curved Wentworth's lips, but he kept his automatic in hand as he made his way to the door. He understood very clearly why General Haley had refused the parole he had offered. Haley knew that he would keep his parole and surrender himself at the day's end; and Haley preferred that Richard Wentworth, alias the Spider, should make good his escape! It was high tribute....

Unmolested, Wentworth made his way swiftly through the halls of the Gibson Hotel until he reached the street. Messengers were roaring away on motorcycles. A truckload of soldiers pounded past. The military already were doing their part, but Wentworth's mouth held a grim line. There was more to it than this. The people would not understand that what was being done was for their own good. In a short while the newspapers and the radio would broadcast the reasons for the evacuation, would urge quiet obedience upon the people. But there would be thousands who would not heed, and other thousands who would try to delay.

There could be no delay! Every second lost in argument might mean the loss of lives, for the military had an impossible feat to perform to clear the city in the short time that was left to them—scarcely more than two hours. Once Tang-akhmut struck, all would be utter confusion. Streets would be blocked by floods of water from bursting mains, by blaring buildings. Panic stampedes would trap other thousands. And, as always, there would be criminals who would strike under the cover of the holocaust.

Wentworth turned sharply away from the door of the hotel and a hand touched his arm. He wheeled sharply and uttered a glad cry.

"Nita!"

Nita was in his arms for a too-brief moment, then they were hurrying away together along the street. General Haley would have to order a search for him and he had already been too long in the vicinity of headquarters.

"I knew I'd find you there, Dick," Nita told him. "What shall we do now? Wait," she said quickly as he started to speak. "Before you say one word! I will not leave your side again!"

Wentworth laughed gaily, "Then I cannot fail!" he cried. His face sobered quickly. "Today, dear, I travel as the Spider! I must get cape and hat, find a car or a horse—a horse would be better—and be everywhere at once. The newspapers made a big to-do over my surrender and for the present there will still be thousands of people who believe in me and who will follow my lead. I should be able to prevent a lot of friction, to speed the exodus all over the city. People must move very rapidly to get out of the city before Tang-akhmut strikes. They will move much more swiftly, if they are led than if they are driven by the soldiers."

While Wentworth spoke, his eyes were busy about him. He found a clothing shop and bade Nita keep watch outside while he made his purchases, a long black raincoat of soft rubber that he wore as a cape upon his shoulders, a wide-brimmed black hat. It was not the costume of the Spider, but it would serve. The world knew his hunch-shouldered silhouette too well to question the identity of the Spider when he proclaimed his identity in this garb. He carried these for the present upon his arm.

Nita got a cab. From an army station, Wentworth commandeered a horse, his authoritative manner overbearing the sergeant's objections… and the grim battle to save Cincinnati began. It would be a desperate battle against odds the Spider dared not calculate. And over it all brooded the shadow of Tangakhmut. If only he could be sure that the man was dead….

CHAPTER 13
THE SPIDER FALLS

MOUNTED ON horseback, with the cape of the Spider swung across the withers, Wentworth turned to the west end of the city. There was a vast area of tenements there, a thick center of population. Both because of the density and because of the flimsy structure of many of the buildings, it was a section of great danger. Even to get the people out of their homes, to start them on their way, would consume most of the time that stretched so narrowly between them and death.

Almost at once Wentworth, with Nita following in the cab, was in the thick of the evacuation. A group of people stood stubbornly at bay before a tenement house. They had been rounded out of the building by soldiers, but they were resisting the order to march. And these soldiers must dash on to other buildings… A gray-haired man stood in the front rank of the little clump, shaking a gnarled fist.

"*Nazis!*" he shouted. "*Nazis!* This a free country iss! Ve vill not our homes leave!"

The soldiers were becoming exasperated. The lieutenant in charge of the platoon was young and he tried to bully… Wentworth swung the cape about his shoulders, rode up steadily. He spoke to the old man in German.

"The enemy is going to burn the city, father," he said quietly. "In less than two hours, *mein herr*. The city must be evacuated!"

The gray head turned toward him, blue eyes that were surprisingly young gazed up at Wentworth.

"I, the Spider, swear this to you!" Wentworth said calmly. "Will you help, *mein herr?* Will you summon others to march?"

The German threw up his arm in salute. He whirled on the people behind him. "Do you not hear what the commandant says? March! Summon others and march!"

Within five minutes, men, women and children were streaming from all the houses into the streets, a thickening tide of them formed and thronged at the heels of Wentworth's horse as he slowly led them farther west. At his urging, people rushed into the tenements to speed the work of the military. The soldiers only needed to march behind, to make sure that buildings were emptied and to speed the progress of the exodus. Wentworth turned in his saddle and smiled into the face of the German who marched stalwartly behind him. Beside the man, a strong-shouldered woman carried her child. Everywhere he looked, faces turned to him, eyes looked to him for leadership.

"A song, *mein herr!*" Wentworth cried. A song…."

At first thinly, then with mounting volume, the song the old German started in his quavering voice gained force; a song that might have seemed strange in any folk less music loving than the Germans. It was the soldier's chorus from Faust that the German chose and the grand swinging rhythm of it swelled in the street. Their step quickened, the march swelled on, and tributary rivers of refugees flowed in from other streets.

When the song was finished, Wentworth stood high in his stirrups. "I go to help others!" he cried. "March on swiftly!"

He spurred the horse ahead, turned a corner, and was gone. Behind him, he heard the deep-throated singing of the marching crowd rise again. The hoofs of another horse sounded behind him and he twisted about. Nita had found a mount and was beside him. She laughed into his face.

"You shan't leave me again!" he cried. But there was no joy in her eyes—and Wentworth remembered her forebodings in the cavern. *Death in the air….*

Farther west they trotted, until the sounds of the singing died behind them. But the march would come through this area. Already, the soldiers had people on the move. Wentworth turned northward into the district called "Over the Rhine."

HE SAW a man spring from a doorway and run swiftly along the street and a few moments later a woman staggered out.

"Thief!" she cried. "Thief! He killed… kill…" She sank to her knees, wrenched by sobs.

Wentworth's gun slid to his palm and he quieted the horse, dropped his sights easily on the target. When he fired, the fugitive spun wildly and crashed against the building wall, rolled over and lay still. Windows flung high, people popped out of doorways.

"A warning to looters!" Wentworth's deep voice rang out. "Any looter will be killed on sight!"

Motionless and silent, the people waited, staring at the caped figure on horseback, at the woman who rode, so gloriously proud, at his side. Wentworth proclaimed the evacuation of the city, told them what threatened.

"You must leave your homes now—at once!" he cried. "Wait for nothing except to carry what food you can lay your hands on! March!"

He turned to the woman who still knelt on the pavement before her shop. The woman had ceased to sob, her eyes clung to Wentworth….

"Come!" he said to her gently, dismounting from his horse. "Come, you must go!"

For a moment the woman shrank back, for a moment she stared back toward the doorway she had left where the thief had killed, then she stumbled to her feet and moved blindly toward Wentworth.

Wentworth mounted her before him on his horse. "This

woman leaves her own dead to help us march!" he called to the people. "Can you do less...."

Presently, Nita found a place for the woman in one of the automobiles that made part of the march and she and Wentworth swung on to seek new followers. The quick response of the people to his summons warmed the Spider's heart; but ever time pressed upon their heels and time meant the difference between life and death. Gradually the denser parts of the city were being cleared; the long lines of refugees filed out into more open country. Wentworth heard sirens wail once off to his left and glimpsed military automobiles speeding northward—the staff cars. That meant Brigadier General Haley had left his headquarters. The sun was almost directly overhead. Within so few minutes the blow would fall—and there was yet more work to be done.

Wentworth whirled to quicken with a song the pace of those who marched densely behind him. A troop of young boys was in the lead. They grinned up at him with worship in their eyes. And there was a steadfast courage in the faces of the men and the women who marched behind them. It was warming, the way their eyes clung to the Spider, the trust in their faces. Looking at them, Wentworth knew in that moment that none of the trials he had undergone, none of the risks he had run was futile. All his life he had served the people, of whom these who marched were a part. It was enough recompense that now a few of the thousands gazed on him with trust in their faces....

He lifted his arms to command a song—and Nita's horse drove against his from the left, while a sledgehammer blow doubled him sharply forward. Far off, thinly as in a dream, he heard the spiteful crack of a high-power rifle!

Rigidly, Wentworth forced himself erect in the saddle. "March on!" he shouted.

HE SET spurs to his horse and crowded the sides of the buildings on his right. He pivoted a corner and felt the strength go out of him, sagged forward in his saddle. No need to ask what had happened. Tang-akhmut had not died! He had struck terribly at the man who was thwarting him in his hour of triumph. There was an agony through Wentworth's back, the warm course of blood across his flesh.

"I saw the powder flash!" Nita cried. "Oh, Dick, Dick... Here, let me help you down."

Wentworth held himself erect by the stiffness of his left arm braced against the withers of his horse. He shook his head weightily.

"You saw the flash... where?"

Nita cried, "Get down, Dick. I don't know now! I couldn't say to save my life. It happened so quickly...."

Wentworth shook his head jerkily. That damned blur before his eyes... When he had gone into Tang-akhmut's hands, he had planned to ask Nita a question, or to learn its answer by search. The fight in the cavern and the pressure of action since then had held him from it. He had to press his mind furiously to make it work... The question....

"Willa Abel," Wentworth whispered, "Do you know... alive or dead?"

"Dead," Nita said swiftly. "I heard Tang-akhmut taunt Clare

with it. Tang-akhmut told Clare she had served him to save a girl who already was dead…."

Wentworth nodded heavily, put his hand to his waist and fumblingly drew a gun. If only the pain in his shoulder would relent… He shut his lips grimly. He would have to wait for the wound to be bandaged. He alighted from his horse and sat on the curb while Nita set to work, tore his shirt to strips and used it. His right shoulder blade had been pierced and the bullet had torn out through the deltoid muscle. Except for the loss of blood and the pain it was not a grave wound. When Nita finished her swift bandaging, Wentworth forced himself to his feet, insisted on mounting.

"Clara Hubbel's apartment," Wentworth said harshly. "It isn't far from here, is it?"

Wentworth was forced to proceed at a walk. Parallel to his progress moved the tramp of feet, the deep rhythm of singing that seemed to lift him along. People marching to safety, but so slowly, so slowly. The fatal hour must be almost at hand….

"Do you think Clare Hubbell is at her home?" Nita demanded finally. "Surely, that can wait, Dick. You've got to get to a doctor."

Wentworth frowned heavily. The street kept swaying before his eyes. He closed them. "There were several explanations possible in the case of Willa Abel," he said, speaking very precisely, for he had to discipline his hazing thoughts. "If she were kidnapped, it might be for the sake of forcing information from her, about the water mains. If that was so, she was kept alive. What you say Tang-akhmut told Clare Hubbell indicates that Clare was led to believe Willa was alive to make Clare serve Tang-akhmut.

Yet I know of no service she did for Tang-akhmut. She tried to escape. She was tortured by him. The reporter, Hal Shields, suggested Willa was dead and that her supposed kidnapping was a blind behind which the Commissioner of Public Works, in charge of water mains, might be hiding. It appears Willa was killed at the very first."

"Then the Commissioner..." Nita hesitated.

Wentworth shook his head, peered about him and reined his horse. He swung heavily to the ground and entered an apartment house. As he went through the door, he heard a distant thud that grew into a concussion, that swelled into a crescendo of noise as of a barrage closing in about him. His lips hardened. His grip on his automatic became hard. He knew what that sound portended. Tang-akhmut's mines had exploded. The water mains of the city were destroyed! Somewhere people were screaming. A fire engine siren began to shriek. Much good they could do against the fiery chemicals of Tang-akhmut!

WENTWORTH MOVED steadily on toward the elevator, Nita beside him. "Dick," she whispered, "we'll be trapped when the fire spreads. We should be leaving the city with all possible speed."

Wentworth nodded. "I want you to wait here...."

Nita said softly, "I won't leave your side, Dick!"

There was no help for it, then. Wentworth entered the elevator and it moved deliberately upward. When he left the elevator, he moved softly, eyes questing about him. The tension drove the weakness from his brain, strengthened him. At Clare's door, he

143

paused only a moment. His automatic bucked twice in his hand and he strode across the threshold.

From a back hallway, a bent old man's figure stumbled forward. "Who are you?" he quavered. "Surely, you don't want me. I am just an old man. I have suffered enough. I am Doctor Abel. Doctor Zachary Abel. They tortured my little girl to death and they stole Clare who was like my daughter...."

It was the rambling voice of a man half-crazed by grief—and Wentworth laughed.

Wentworth laughed and leveled his automatic.

"It was you who tortured Willa," he said harshly. "And you who have destroyed the city, Tang-akhmut! But your time has come!"

The aged man dropped on his knees and Nita's hand touched Wentworth's arm timidly.

"Dick, what are you saying?" she whispered. "This man can't be Tang-akhmut!"

Wentworth laughed again. "It is Tang-akhmut! He killed Dr. Abel, so that he could take his place. That was the reason Willa was slain, too, and Clare Hubbell intimidated by being told that Willa was held hostage. This was the way Clare served Tang-akhmut. Don't you see the cleverness of the man? When he had finished with his looting of the city, he wanted to disappear quietly, both from his own men and from the knowledge of mankind. Who would look for Tang-akhmut in the identity of the man Tang-akhmut had chiefly wronged? Who would think that Dr. Abel, whose daughter was murdered by Tang-akhmut and whose niece was tortured, could possibly be Tang-akhmut?

Probably, Tang-akhmut came first to get information from Willa Abel, then he saw the possibilities of the situation...."

From somewhere in the apartment, a girl's voice lifted shrilly. "Help, help, Spider!" she cried. "A bomb...."

Wentworth took a step forward and the aged doctor sprang agilely aside through a doorway.

His laughter—and it was the deep mocking laughter of Tang-akhmut—came back terribly.

"Escape if you can, Wentworth," he cried. "This house is mined. Within seconds, you all shall die!"

Wentworth fired twice toward the doorway, went past it in a leap that hurled him, weak and almost fainting, against the door from behind which Clare had cried. He lunged through it. On a table between Clare and Adam Peck, who sagged unconscious in his bonds, was a tubular piece of metal attached to a rude clock detonator.

The hands... Good God, already they were almost in contact with the explosion point.

From behind him, Nita cried out swiftly.

"The fire escape, Dick! He's escaping down the fire escape!"

Wentworth let his automatic fall from his hand, snatched the bomb and whirled to the window. He scarcely felt the gash of glass in his arm as he hurled the thing downward. He reeled back, groping for his weapon, and realized it was back near the table on the floor. He reached for it, bracing his good shoulder against the table—

Outside, a man screamed terribly, in awful fear, the voice of Tang-akhmut! A moment later, there was a subdued explosion, then flame sheeted upward past the broken window. Wentworth seized his gun and moved heavily back toward the opening, peered downward. On the steel fire escape landing two floors below, something wrapped in flames was twisting and writhing terribly.

Wentworth had not planned this thing, but Heaven knew that it was just the man should die so, tortured as he had tortured so many others. It was just, but… Slowly, Wentworth aimed his automatic. He squeezed the trigged until the hammer clicked on an empty chamber and the screaming below had ceased. Wentworth lifted his eyes from the dead man. The horizon was spotted with the smoke of a dozen fires, but they were mostly in the thicker downtown area which he had evacuated. Vast sections of the city would be destroyed, but the people were safe and their enemy, who lay below, was dead. Tang-akhmut would never again bring his Terror to mankind.

Wentworth turned away from the window. He felt empty, drained, despite the joy of ultimate victory. He was still a hunted man. He must flee before his presence was discovered….

Clare was gazing on him. Peck had recovered consciousness and there was that in his eyes which warmed Wentworth's heart anew. And Nita was beside Wentworth, her arm supporting him. Wentworth smiled….

"You will tell them that Tang-akhmut is dead," he said quietly. "And tell them that…."

Adam Peck said deeply, "I shall tell them that Richard Wentworth is the bravest man the world has ever known. I shall tell them that if he is the Spider, then I shall admire and respect the

Spider all the days of my life! I shall tell them that the Spider is beyond man's law as he has this day fulfilled the law of God!"

Wentworth felt almost happy when he and Nita stole from the building and slipped away through the chaotic city. It was good to have the respect of a brave man, and the love of a brave woman… His good arm tightened about Nita.